CAROLS
and
SP🔑ES

Winter Stories

Collection, The First
JENNIFER KROPF

ISBN Ebook: 978-1-990555-26-8
ISBN Paperback: 978-1-990555-27-5
ISBN Hardcover: 978-1-990555-28-2

I'd like to dedicate this book to my siblings,
Steph, Melis, and Jesse.

Weirdos.

A
BLEND
OF
HARMONIES

Novella, The First

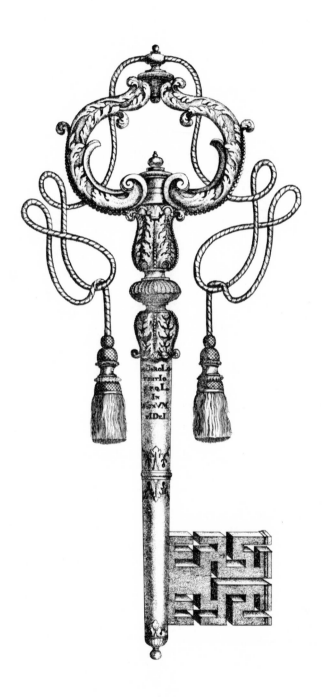

FIRSTLY

Certain things always happened to Charlie Little. Silly, unusual things. Things that ought not to have occurred. And they always related to music.

Up in the trees, wind would brush the leaves into a whispering shuffle, a clatter of branches and greens not worth a glance to most. But to Charlie, the wind always brought a tune with it; a low hum most frequently, only climbing to a higher pitch when it slipped through a tiny space. The evergreens sang the highest—their airy songs of pinesap belonging to the heavens and the stars. The tune that lifted from their bristles by the galloping gusts added to the choir of moaning trunks and shuddering breeze-tunnels harmonizing with musical ribbons. Even the leaves clapped their praises, a special rhythm to propel the melodies onward.

The first time young Charlie Little hummed along with the symphony of the woodlands, he was tucked beneath a thin quilt of fastened rags in his stick-and-mortar home. He caught the pitch and strengthened the note with a whistle.

As the icy breezes slipped into his home through the twig walls, they carried the boy's voice across his room and out into the hallway, melting every frozen thing in its path. And this was a strange occurrence indeed, for it was the coldest night of the season—Charlie's mother was shivering beneath a knit shawl, and his father was boiling water for tea, clutching the kettle with blue fingers. Their middle-aged bones had shuddered like sticks until Charlie sang, and then it was as though the boy had drawn the heat right up from the floor.

It was the first clue that something was not quite as it should be with that boy.

On another day, the wind's bitter howls raged through the house, shattering windows and bringing a clamour of shrieks into the cottage along with a prickling chill. But Charlie sang it away, as though the ruckus was no more than a nuisance needing a reminder to hush.

Things of this sort occurred a time or three, making Charlie's parents wonder if they had missed something important on the eve he had been born. They had heard of children with specialties—odd talents that could be used for great things. But never had they thought their son would be among the talented ones.

It was not clear what Charlie sang about, or what he sang to, only that something within him drove him to praise, even when the days were hard. He was a boy always found with a smile, a twinkle in his eye, and a trot in his step. Many on the Little's dirt street knew of Charlie, for he brought laughter to even the grumpiest of old men.

At first Charlie's parents were delighted, inviting their neighbours in to keep warm on bitter days when the polar winds breathed across Bellbun. They celebrated with tea and biscuits, which Charlie's mother would bake by the dozen.

This had gone on for a blissful measure of five seasons plus a quarter before word reached Charlie's mother and father about another little girl with a similar gift. Her name was Melody Carol, and Charlie was her senior by several seasons. The King of the Pines had sought out young Miss Carol for her voice and had recruited her to join the Evergreen Host: the highest and most elite division of war bloods in the entirety of the Green Kingdom.

"How can this be?" Charlie's mother had asked the one who delivered the gossip—a young teenager who swore his name was Edward Haid. Edward was a boy who always seemed to be hiding something. Charlie often played catch with him in the meadow clearing when the wind was right, and the sun refused to be bashful, and the clouds held in their snow.

Edward regularly passed through Bellbun in slacks, a plain tunic, and a fur coat. But this time, Edward had arrived cloaked in an emerald-green cape clasped by shiny silver clips; something he had never worn in front of the Little family before.

Charlie crept forward to spy, hoping to remain unnoticed. The customary flint of humour was absent from Edward's face and Charlie could not understand why.

"Melody Carol is just a little girl!" Charlie's father roared while Charlie listened from the hallway. "They cannot really plan to turn a little girl into a soldier?"

"I'm unmerrily ubbersnugged by the king's choices," Edward said. "I only came to warn you because Charlie is my friend, and I love this quiet town and your family. You gave me a place to escape the cold when I wished to avoid my home and duties. I will not forget that no matter what happens next." Edward rubbed his pink-veined eyes, giving Charlie the impression he had spent the night running to deliver this news.

"And how did you come to know this in the first place, Edward? How did you learn what the king has done with the girl?" Mrs. Little's tone held a pinch of skepticism.

There was a pause during which Charlie watched Edward shuffle on the front step. He thought to swoop in and save his friend who had come to warn him and now stood trial before Mrs. Little for it.

"It's a long story. One I will not bore you with," Edward replied. "But I wished to let you know before the Evergreen Host shows up to take Charlie. Natter about him will reach the king in a measure, I'm sure."

Another beat of silence hung in the air before Edward spoke again. "Just know that the king did not hear about Charlie from me." Edward nodded to Mr. and Mrs. Little and backed away from the home of twigs and forest brush.

For a good measure of quarters after, Charlie's parents kept him inside. He watched his mother stitch modest dresses with her dexterous fingers. The talented gownmaker always created the loveliest chiffon and beaded satin gowns she could never afford to keep, with pea-sized bells and soft fringes, ruched bodices, and puddle skirts.

It was only on the days Charlie could sneak out that he was able to roam the streets, sliding over the ice on his boots and ducking the ever-present observation of the Evergreen Host that seemed to have migrated to his little town of Bell-bun in large supply.

The kingdom's lush smells soaked the air when the wind was quiet: the smoking meat over open-pit flames, the crisp-crust breads in ovens, and the sour juices from ripe iceber-ries. The feasts of the Green Kingdom never ceased, unless the storms grew too bothersome to stay outdoors and all were forced to separate to their homes.

A quarter after Charlie's ten plus seventh season of age, Charlie sneaked from his home while his mother was away and his father was out chopping firewood in the forest with the woodsmen.

Charlie's golden eyes wandered over the folk in the street wearing scowls rather than the smile of melting butter on bread that warmed Charlie's features. He was recognized by a townsfolk or three; his mother's fabric supplier nodded Charlie's way, and the bird farmer who passed by in a hurry did the same.

At the end of the stone-walled street, a storm rolled in. The snowflakes twinkled and twirled and arched in a weave, drawing Charlie's brows to burrow. He had the strangest thought—that perhaps someone was bringing this storm up from the earth *on purpose*.

With a quizzical look, Charlie watched the bird farmer reach the Evergreen Bank of Rings at the end of the road—a place where a baby slept soundly in a basket on the front porch, and an old woman rocked back and forth in a chair to watch over it.

The storm would be awfully chilly for them when it poured over the street.

Charlie rushed to where the graying woman swayed with her eyes closed, and he pulled the blanket up to the baby's chest so the yarn brushed her chin. He was not supposed to sing anymore, at least, not outside the house. But he did not think his parents would mind if he did it to help a baby.

Turning to face the hand of ice and wind curling over the forest, Charlie began in a high whirr, something that tickled the bottom of his throat. Slowly, he let the tune rise into a song, and he hummed the first melody that came to his mind, one that seemed to drift up from the moss and the bark and the roots and the rain, into his ears and out of his mouth.

As the wordless ballad left his lips, Charlie watched the chain of flakes unclasp overhead and drift into a sprinkling of dust, carpeting the muddy street floors in patches. The winds shut their mouths and the cold melted away, revealing the log-stacked shops at the end of the road that had been entirely consumed only a moment ago.

With a glance, Charlie shot a satisfied smile to the sleeping baby who would now remain undisturbed. But when he turned back toward his home, he found his fellow folk of Bellbun staring in dismay.

The bird farmer. The fabric supplier. All the rest of them, too.

Past them, a girl stood in the street in a green coat that reached her ankles. She appeared young and sweet, ginger and fair, with wide olivine eyes. But anger flushed her face, for it seemed this little girl had not been bested before.

She was the one who had summoned the storm—Charlie was not sure how he knew, but he was quite certain. A rare gift stirred behind those furious olivine eyes. And Charlie had silenced her storm with nothing more than a hum.

Around the fair girl, ten plus five equipped soldiers of the Evergreen Host gripped axes and spears in glittering fury.

SECONDLY

"What have you done, Charlie?" his mother asked with a flush. Even when she scolded him compassion burned in the corners of her eyes, for she dearly appreciated that her son had tried to help a baby. But even so, Charlie had not kept his voice quiet as he had been told.

A silly smile took Charlie's mouth. He did not regret his lullaby for the child. And, naturally, his infectious spirit spread to his mother.

"This is not funny, Charlie," she whispered, even though she was smiling now also.

The front door swung open and in rushed Charlie's father, a bead of sweat clinging to his temple.

"They're here for him. The Evergreen Host has come for Charlie!" His voice resembled a shrieking morningbird, bringing Charlie half a step back.

"What does this mean?" Charlie felt words of a song bubble up in his chest. He kept his mouth closed though, for singing was what had gotten him into this muddle in the first place.

But his father shook his head. "Run, Charlie! Hide in the forest! I will come find you when they're gone!"

Charlie's stare flickered between his mother and his father. The memory of the girl in the street with the draping green coat stole his thoughts—and her dreaded song which had summoned the storm to sweep over Bellbun.

She was what his parents did not want him to become.

Charlie rushed out the back door of their home of twigs, leaving the clatter of the door in his wake.

It did not take Charlie long to get lost in the woods. He had stumbled this way and that, around a bend or three. Charlie did not realize he was following a soft trail of sound until he reached the catacombs—a place he had been only once before, a long measure of time ago.

A distorted, gray stone face stared back at him, built into a mosaic of rock that plugged the tunnel. The gentle hum of a hundred trickling rivers and the applause of swaying wheat-berry stalks seeped through the cracks from the inside, tickling Charlie's ears and summoning him to test the strength of the barricade.

In a younger season of his timestring, Charlie had sat on his bed beneath a bundle of tossed blankets while his father told him ancient stories of things that had been forbidden to speak of in the Green Kingdom for nearly twenty seasons— stories pressed into a quiet sleep while the King of the Pines waged war upon the Crimson King. The wild tales had not always been forbidden. In fact, the stories of the ancient times used to be treasured—stored here in these catacombs, preserved for the future generations of the kingdom. Now every influence of the ancient tales was sealed shut by rock and plaster.

Staring at the goliath of stone, Charlie wondered if perhaps his father did not mean for him to venture this far. He wondered if he should wait until his father figured out where he had gone.

The frigid day numbed Charlie's thumbs as he twiddled them. He paced—crunching footprints into the snow in a repetitive pattern until the ground around him boasted a wide, pressed-down oval.

Finally, Charlie stopped again by the entrance of the catacombs where he had started.

He brushed his fingers over the nearest rocks, feeling the coarse texture beneath his cold fingertips. It was shut solid, but Charlie swore he could hear a low echo in the dense throats of the thickest boulders.

With a tilt of his head, he leaned in to press his ear against the chilly stone. It was just a hiss, almost too subtle to hear, but from deep within, a bass plucked its strings. And suddenly Charlie felt silly for not having the thought to listen from the beginning.

Such a spinbug, he was.

The boy quieted his curiosity and closed his eyes. Breeze kissed his flesh, flirting its way through his hair as the sweet voices of the wind rose behind him. Were these low-humming rocks singing along with the airy flutes of the woods? Was this spirited, twirling breeze dancing to their praises?

In a sweet refrain, Charlie found a tune drifting from his lips. He sang along with the glories in his midst because he could not help himself now that he was listening.

As his voice climbed to a stronger tune, the drumming of the rocks grew louder. Charlie pulled his head away, staring at the barrier in amazement. He scrambled back, for he knew a great thing was about to happen.

A loud crack hissed in the air, and the rocks *burst*. Flakes of boulders sprang in every direction, chunks rolling away and landing with thuds. The mortar crumbled like sand, piling into heaps on the snowy floor until all that stood before Charlie was the windy mouth of a dark, open tunnel.

He beheld the music...an ancient yuletide carol hidden away below the other sounds-- quenched by the loud war drums of the Evergreen Host, the clatter of cutlery, and the bellowing of feasting citizens across the kingdom.

Charlie inched forward, weaving through the littered rocks. A new wind—icy and rebellious—tugged at his clothes in a feeble attempt to keep him in its grips, but Charlie would not be so easily convinced by the cold.

He was barely through the entrance when the dark tunnel burst into an array of bright lights like crystal stars. A new room encompassed him, sweeping in like a wave off the snowseas and glowing with droplets of colour.

A labyrinth of shelves swallowed half the space. Tables were tucked into crevices wherever they could fit, decorated with copper trinkets in glass displays. Dried flowers hung from string above, all threading toward a chandelier of lanterns, candles, and blossoms knotted together with braids of silken white ribbon.

It was as though Charlie had stepped into another world.

The entrance of the catacombs was gone, and before him was a room smelling of fresh gardens and old paper, warm icing and hot cinnamon-sprinkled apples. And soft melodies...they circled in the space, though Charlie was sure they were not coming from any instrument.

When he turned to gape at the magnificent rose-pink lights, Charlie spotted a man emerging from the labyrinth of bookshelves with a scroll tucked beneath his arm.

The fellow was young, like Charlie, with brilliant four-toned eyes, soft features, and bronze skin. Scars glowed on his wrists, visible by how his tunic was rolled up at the elbows.

The song in the room promised the young man was safe. *Safe*. That was the only word Charlie wanted to sing now, but he swallowed his song and bit his lips together, certain it would be odd to carol so unexpectedly to the fellow.

Humour lit the young man's face as though he had heard Charlie's thoughts.

"Season's greetings." Charlie made sure the remark came out as simple words, with no tune whatsoever.

"Greetings, Charlie Little," the fellow replied. "I am the one called Elowin. A name from the beginning, and a name for the end."

In truth, Charlie had never heard the name *Elowin* upon any folk's lips before now. But somehow, he was sure he had always known it. But how did this man know Charlie's name?

"Your enemies will not find you here." Elowin set his scroll down on a table, scuffing the elbows of his white tunic.

"Where is here?" Charlie asked, glancing back at where the entrance of the catacombs had once been.

"This is a library." Elowin raised a hand to the room as though it should have been obvious.

Charlie stole another look at the books and shelves.

"Am I still in the catacombs?"

Another smile found the young man's face. "Yes and no. You are where the catacombs are, but those who do not believe cannot find this place. They see only abandoned tunnels and torn pages, all that is left of their once-Truth. A true reflection of their souls."

Elowin drifted to another table and picked up a book with copper edges. When he flipped it open, Charlie noticed that the words inside were the red colour of sweet maples. As soon as Charlie saw them, he could hear the words of their story in his ears.

"How did I get in here?" Charlie asked.

"I brought you here," Elowin said.

"For what? The music?" Charlie guessed.

Elowin's eyes flickered up, revealing the lush forest greens, sparkling silvers, and deep ocean-purples in his irises. They were unlike any eyes Charlie had seen.

"Not quite," the young man replied. "There is another reason I brought you, Charlie. She will be here soon." Elowin closed the book, quieting the story, and rested it back on the table.

"*She...?*"

Echoes of sharp panting and pounding footsteps filled the bookshelf maze. A girl propelled through a set of shelves, knocking a book or three to the floor. She whirled in surprise at the noise she had made, nearly stumbling over her own feet. But she skipped to run again, until she pulled up her gaze and saw Charlie there. She halted, the heels of her boots skidding along the floor, tassels of fair blonde hair hanging over her face as panic forged her gray eyes to metal.

But that was not what struck Charlie most of all.

This girl wore *red*. A cascading crimson dress adorned her small figure, twinkling rubies hugged her earlobes, and rosette bulbs covered her long sleeves. He nearly choked.

Never in his life had Charlie Little seen a Red with his own eyes. And he was certain that was what she was—a Red.

"Who…Where am I?" The girl's gray eyes swam with distrust until her stare fell upon Elowin, and at the sight of him, they softened.

But it was short-lived. When her glance rounded back to Charlie, her silvery eyes sharpened back to war blades.

Charlie held up his hands at his own defense. "I did not bring you here," he promised.

Only then did he notice the green cuffs wrapping his black coat—a set once belonging to his father. Charlie dropped his hands and clasped them behind his back.

"I…I was running through the palace, to the…" The girl looked back the way she had come, to the shelf made empty where she had hurtled the innocent books from their perch.

"To the museum?" Elowin guessed.

That brought her attention back.

"Yes…That's where I meant to go. Not…" the girl waved her hand around, "here."

"Well, isn't that strange." Elowin's face held a smirk when he glanced at Charlie.

An unexpected smile leaked into Charlie's expression. He unhooked his fingers to let his hands fall back to his sides.

But the girl's stare found his cuffs again. Then it climbed his coat to the green stitching in his collar, and down his sleeves to the green patch his mother had sewn over the worn spot on his elbow.

"She's a *Red*," he finally observed aloud.

"You're wearing green," she said back.

Charlie and the girl had spoken at the same time. Though Elowin was there, it seemed they could only look at each other now. Charlie, being a Green Kingdom merchant with a dangerous secret talent, and her, a Red Kingdom dweller, and from the *palace* of all places, with all her glittering jewels.

"This is your introduction, and with it comes a responsibility—one you both may have felt approaching for a measure." Elowin picked up the book again, the same one he had been reading with the red letters. He cradled it in his arm and moved to the labyrinth of shelves. His voice was so melodic, Charlie almost missed the words as they twirled and dipped.

"Wait…you're leaving *now?*" he finally sputtered.

"You will have to figure out a thing or three for yourself, Charlie Little. Follow the music and don't be afraid to believe. I'm never far, and my messengers will look out for you." He stole a glance at the girl as he said it.

With that, Elowin disappeared around a curve of shelves, leaving Charlie with the girl and the scent of old books.

A pinch of silence passed between them.

Reaching down to straighten her dress, the Red girl sniffed.

"I don't trust you, Green." She said it before she even lifted her head to look upon him again. Her light hair was in tangles, but Charlie could not keep himself from noticing she was quite pretty.

"I don't think I trust you either," he admitted.

15

He took in a deep breath to muster his courage and marched across the room to close the cavern between them. The girl's eyes narrowed, possibly an instrument of defense to keep him at bay, but it would not work on Charlie. He extended his hand, his green cuff blatant under the multicoloured lighting of the room.

"I'm Charlie. Charlie Little."

The girl clung to an odd look as she studied his hand, but after a moment she took it. Her skin was soft from whatever Red Kingdom oils she was accustomed to, and it brought a strange smile to Charlie's face. He was not sure why.

"I'm Cora Thimble." Her voice was milk and sugar.

THIRDLY

Charlie found himself whistling on his walk home. After he had wandered from the catacombs and been blanketed by the scents of pine needles and moist bark, the air had turned frosty, and the slush had crisped to ice. But he hardly noticed. The sky was gray, a solid colour with only a few speckles of light, just like Cora Thimble's eyes.

Skipping up his front steps, he pushed his way inside the house with his musical mind left in another place. But he halted in the kitchen.

From the Little family's round wood table, his mother's stare catapulted upwards. On either side of her, men in black uniforms and emerald green capes glanced at him also.

His mother yelled, "*Run*, Charlie!"

But how could he leave his mother alone with these men? An axe was strapped to the closest one's back.

He hesitated.

"*Ruuuun!*"

The breath escaped Charlie's lungs at her scream, and he backpedaled down his front steps, spinning back toward the catacombs.

Ice crunched under his feet as he raced. Behind him, the boots of the Host pounded against the snow—fast men, trained to move like water and wind—but they did not know the turns of Bellbun as Charlie did, and they did not know where he was going.

Charlie dug his heel in a sharp turn, barely ducking a rope net cast in his direction.

His legs drove him up the hill at the edge of town and into the thick woods where he could outrun the Host with a measure of luck.

Sweat licked his back moments later as he slid to the entrance of the catacombs. The name of the young man he had met there was on his lips when he paused and looked upon the entrance in dismay.

The stones had returned. The catacombs were plugged once again.

Charlie's fingers brushed the rocks held tightly together with mortar. He knew they had broken, yet here they were. But there had not been time for anyone to rebuild the blockage in the short hour he had been away.

With a glance over his shoulder, Charlie approached the plug of stones and pressed his hands against it. Nothing would budge. He heaved his shoulder against the stone.

"Elowin!" he called at the catacombs.

Moving back a step, Charlie wondered if he was going mad.

The sounds of a marching army lifted from the depths of the woods.

With a huff, Charlie returned to the plug, closing his eyes when nothing else worked. He did not have time to listen for the music. All he could hear was the clanging of silver armour and stomping upon the earth. They were too close; he was out of time.

An anxious noise escaped Charlie's lips as he turned to face his fate, to embrace the flashes of emerald capes that could now be seen through the trunks. It seemed Charlie would discover soon enough why the king wanted him so badly.

Something tickled his throat. Charlie slapped the side of his neck, thinking it to be a spinbug, but the tickle turned into a warm sensation that spread up into his mouth, taking his lips. Realizing, Charlie looked back at the plug of the catacombs. He took in a deep breath and blew upon the wall of rock with a simple breath.

It was enough.

Mortar cracked and crumbled, and a great shiver rumbled the soil below Charlie's feet. He watched in awe as fragments of rock fell out from their places like before, crumbling away to reveal the dark tunnel behind.

Either Charlie truly had gone mad, or perhaps he was more gifted than he knew. The thought made him steal one last glance at the Evergreen Host with their axes and bows. A smirk took Charlie's mouth as he turned to jog into the catacombs. He ran deep into the tunnel until he could no longer see a thing.

"Elowin?" he called.

Hoarse shouts and the low shrieks of axes smashing debris at the entrance drove Charlie to spin around. But his lack of focus cost him; his toe caught the sprout of a rock, and he tumbled.

A brightness encompassed him. It was as though he had fallen into a pool of light.

Charlie tumbled onto a polished, spotless cream floor with a long narrow rug down its middle.

A *red* rug.

The dark catacombs had vanished, and he found himself in another place.

When Charlie lifted his gaze, he beheld dense sculptures lining sparkling walls, vivid crimson drapes tracing ruby glass petals in stained-glass windows, and silken maroon paints brushed into murals upon the rounded teardrop ceilings.

The rhythms of his chest were not that of a song now, but of something much more dreadful. Of all the corners of the globe, this was the cruelest place Charlie could have fallen into.

Charlie Little, the son of a green woodsman, was certain he had just found himself in the Red Kingdom.

FOURTHLY

A soldier in a copper helmet appeared. He blinked down at Charlie for a pinch then drew his sword. Charlie hardly had time to pull himself into a roll before he would have met iron. The silver blade sliced the red carpet, putting a fresh hole in the tufts.

"Spy!" the soldier sang to the masses beyond the hall.

Charlie scrambled on his hands—still damp from the catacomb rocks—rubbing a path of dirt along the floor. The guard sprang, forcing Charlie to duck into another roll where he came up onto his feet and broke into a race.

He twisted into a narrow hallway of gold-rimmed glass mirrors and slipped onto a balcony beyond. There were so many hallways to choose from and so many sparkling furnishings and ornaments that made him stand out in his green threads.

At a curve, satin drapes covered a window. Without

thinking, Charlie grabbed the fabric and pulled himself behind, disappearing into the folds. He stifled his breathing as guards trotted mere inches from where he stood.

When the hallway returned to its still slumber, Charlie mustered the courage to peer around the drapes. Old rumours of this kingdom's cruelty played through his mind, but every thought came to a halt when his golden eyes landed on the painting hanging proudly across the hall. The artwork depicted a man with black hair, copper armour, and a tall, jewel-studded crown. A crown that had the royal crest stamped into its rim. A crown *anyone* from *any* kingdom of the snow globe would know.

Charlie had not found himself in just any Red Kingdom chateau. He was in the *palace* of the *Crimson King*—the very monarch the King of the Pines raged against in a deadly war. The king of the very Reds who captured Greens for wicked entertainment. And vicious games. And severe punishments.

And now the Reds knew a Green was here.

For an insufferable measure, Charlie had ducked from one hiding place to the next, growing as still and quiet as an ashworm every time Ruby Legionnaires marched by. He had abandoned his green cuffs, torn off the green patch from his elbow, and folded down the collar of his tunic to hide the treacherously coloured threading at his neckline.

It took the full measure of his scampering for his heart to settle.

When he slipped into a darkened room, Charlie found rows upon rows of exquisite costumes: smooth beads, soft feathers, silk blossoms, and intricate lace all stitched together to form gowns and vests, coats and hats—an assortment that may have been used for recitals and theatrical purposes to amuse the royals.

He grabbed a garment but hesitated. Putting on a red robe was an act of treason to the Green Kingdom—punishable by imprisonment, or worse. If the Council of the Pines ever discovered how Charlie's fingers grazed the scarlet satin clinging to silver hangers, Charlie would be in a great deal of trouble.

But he was also in trouble now.

Quickly, Charlie rummaged through the costumes, passing by everything that glittered and glistened, pushing away items with ruffles or gemstones. He hastened until he found a simple wine-red vest with copper details. It would not hide the hole in his sleeve, but perhaps he could make it work anyway.

Charlie skipped over to the mirror as he pulled it on, and once deeming the vest worthy, he rolled his sleeves to his elbows to hide the tear in the smothering folds. He ruffled his hair back into place and even flashed himself a smile.

It was all quite silly. There was no reason for him to be happy about any of it. But he could not wipe the grin from his face at the sight of himself in such lustrous silk, and in a forbidden colour, no less.

Charlie moved for the door, opening it a sliver to peek out. He was not sure if his disguise was clever enough.

Unfortunately, he had no friends in the Red Kingdom, and no one to tell him which way was in, or out, or up, or down in this palace of curved hallways and warped mirrors and twisted marble stairs. The only Red Kingdom dweller he had ever encountered in his whole timestring was Cora Thimble.

The palace was speckled with Ruby Legion capes by the time Charlie had tracked her down. He had been forced to ask a servant for Cora by name, and in doing so, he was terribly worried he had given himself away. But the servant—a stout elf with an oversized claret bowtie—waved him towards a door at the top of a staircase where light spilled from a crack.

"Thank you kindly," Charlie said in his politest tune. That had drawn the servant's brow to an arch, and Charlie considered the servants were perhaps not treated so pleasantly in the palace.

He trotted up the stairs with a bothersome clamour from his weighty forest boots, and he peered both ways down the great hall. The only source of life was from the room where the elf-servant had pointed.

A wispy, floral pattern laced across the heavy door clinging to shiny iron hinges. Biting his lips, Charlie drifted close enough to see in without being seen.

The whispers of four sputtlepun girls fluttered out to meet him from where they rested at the foot of a glorious cream bed with delicate chiffon shades dangling from its rafters. Charlie's pulse skipped when he realized Cora Thimble was indeed among them.

She appeared different now than the dampened, flustered

girl she had been when she first ran into Elowin's library. Her golden hair was brushed and smooth as ribbons, cascading by her face where her gray eyes glistened like the sparkling silver powder on her lids. Her dress was formal—an empire-waisted thing with layered organza down to her ankles.

Swallowing his nerves and biting back another strange smile, Charlie moved into the doorway and knocked a soft beat against the doorframe.

The pebble talk in the room had risen; giggles exploded into a feminine song of suds and sparks, and no one inside heard him. So, Charlie cleared his throat loudly.

It seemed all these girls were deaf.

"Cora!" Charlie's call rang through the room like a clanging bell, bringing all the banter and bubbles to a halt.

Cora Thimble glanced up. Her moondust eyes landed on Charlie and her rosy cheeks drained of colour. Unsure of what else to do, Charlie waved.

Cora lifted from the bed in a hurry and marched through the room with that same dagger-sharp gaze. She reached Charlie—shoving him back out to the hall by the palm of her hand—and pulled the door shut behind her.

The look on her face said enough, accusing him of all sorts of dreadful things, her shaking hands and pale cheeks speaking volumes.

"I ended up here on accident. I was scuttling through the catacombs," Charlie tried to explain in hushed tones.

"The catacombs? What are the catacombs?" Cora Thimble's voice was spice and salt now. "Never mind," she huffed, the flush leaking back into her skin. She took his hand and hauled him to a room down the hall, only to push him in ahead of her.

She certainly did a lot of pushing.

Charlie glanced around at the space littered with jewelry and porcelain as the click of the shutting door broke the silence.

Gold rings and trinkets were everywhere—a brush on the dresser, a hand mirror on the soft-sheeted bed, bone-white pearls spilling from the mouth of a bronze box on the fireplace mantle. But the most notable things were all the keys. Some were no larger than Charlie's pinky finger, others as big as branches with unusual, hooked ends. Shiny brass, dark copper, matte bronze, rose gold, pale silver, black iron, pearly steel…there were so many colours. They rested in discarded piles upon every surface, some hanging by a long thread along the window like a decoration.

A rocking chair filled the corner of the space, a closed book on the table beside it with a cloth tongue poking out to mark the page. A porcelain mug hosted the remains of old tea.

"Is this your room?" he guessed.

"Don't speak, Charlie Little," Cora scolded. So, Charlie shut his mouth.

She came around and gazed at him; his new red vest, his lack of green.

"I still do not trust you," she said, though her shoulders relaxed a pinch. "But I will admit that a thing or three draws me to you. A thing that is the work of Elowin, I think."

At the mention of that name, Charlie straightened. "You seem to know more about Elowin than I do," he realized. "Who is he, exactly?" Charlie could think of nothing else now. All of this was still unexplained, especially how he had gotten here.

"I asked you not to speak," Cora said, but she drew in a deep breath and paused to think with a flutter of her lashes. "I'm not quite certain how I know Elowin. I hadn't seen him in person until the moment I also met you. But I've had ten plus two dreams this last quarter during which I spoke with someone about…" She glanced off. "I have been having visions, too," she said, changing direction. "And they're not by Red Kingdom magic. Elowin is different than our prophets and spellcasters, I'm certain of it." Cora mustn't have realized she was pacing, drifting over the tiles toward the fireplace. She picked up a loose bead and stared at it. "He does not walk in the shadows as they do." Her voice was quiet as though she spoke to herself now.

So, she didn't know Elowin more than Charlie. Just through dreams, as Charlie was becoming sure he knew Elowin through songs. What a strange connection this all was.

"And what did he speak to you of in your dreams?" Charlie pressed, tempting her to tell him to be quiet again.

Cora's stare turned silver and sharp. "I do not believe that is for you to know."

His face soured. That did not seem fair.

A knock shuddered the door and Charlie's heart punched forward.

"They cannot know I'm here," he whispered, pestering her for help. He could not imagine what the Red Kingdom royals would do to him if he, a Green, was caught in their palace.

With a pause and a gold-lashed blink, Cora reluctantly took Charlie by his rolled-up sleeve and ushered him to her closet. He dove into the racks of hanging dresses, brushed by smooth and itchy fabrics, and turned to see Cora slide the door shut to seal him in. Her eyes hovered on him through the grates for a moment before she turned and went to meet whoever had knocked.

"Season's greetings, Miss Thimble. I trust you're merry?" An airy voice of a man Charlie could not see curled into the room. As Charlie shifted to spy, a gem broke free from the nearest dress and bounced across the closet floor with a clatter, freezing his heart.

Cora's stare flickered toward the closet, and a man's head in a gold helmet poked around to glance into the room.

"I'm cleaning, Sir Mahogonot. My belongings are in a shameful state of mutiny. I do not wish for anyone to enter my quarters in this condition," Cora admitted, dragging her gaze back to the guard.

"Yes, of course, but you should know a Pine spy was spotted in the palace—a young sputtlepun as strong as a polar bear," he swore, and Charlie slapped a hand over his mouth to smother a laugh. "Be on your guard, Miss Thimble. If you see even a thread of green, shout for us immediately. We will come rescue you." The guard pulled himself, and his helmet, back into the hall.

"I will, indeed. Thank you for checking on me, Sir Mahogonot." Cora shut the door with a slow sweep and turned the lock.

Instantly, Charlie pushed himself from the closet, for the air inside was growing thin. With him came a dress or three, unlatching from their hangers and tumbling to the floor in heaps of liquid satin.

"Sorry." Charlie stooped to retrieve them all in a single

armful. Crinoline blossomed by his face, bringing on rapid blinking when it poked his eyes.

"Are you unable to keep yourself together for even a few seconds, Green?" Cora's scolding was a sound Charlie was getting used to hearing.

"I said I was sorry." He dumped the gowns back in the closet. With a quick swish, he rolled the closet doors together before the dresses might tumble out again.

It was not orderly, but she had, after all, claimed she was in the process of cleaning her room.

Cora bit down on a scowl. "You are not a nobleman. That much is certain," she remarked as she sashayed to the window, her organza whispering across the floor.

Charlie could not decide if the comment was meant as an insult.

"So, can you march me out of here or what?" he said, moving on.

But Cora glanced back at him, startled. "You want to leave?"

"Well, of course. Why wouldn't I? I'm a peg out of its shell here." Charlie stole a look at her closed door.

"But Elowin brought you to this palace. It must be for a reason," Cora objected. "Kingsblood, don't you even wish to discover what that reason is?" She folded her arms.

A glimmer of silver soared by Cora's window. A bird— white with touches of silver upon its wings. Even through the thick glass of her rosebud stained-glass window, Charlie could hear the bird singing a merry song.

"What can I do in this scotchy kingdom where everyone is Red and I'm Green? Maybe I was sent here to fetch you. Maybe you are meant to come to Green with me."

"To the Green Kingdom?" Suddenly Cora laughed. Her laugh was high and beautiful and flirtatious. "I'm a noble-woman of the Crimson Court. They would have terrible ideas of what to do with me in your kingdom," she promised, but her face changed. "And I could not leave them behind." Her sharp eyes aimed away as she lost herself to her own thoughts.

"You have a family?" Charlie guessed.

"Not my family. My friends—the ones you saw. They're mindswept, just like everyone else here." Cora headed for the rocking chair and tugged a burgundy cloak off the back spindles. "That is why I cannot leave, Charlie Little. Because if I go, there will be no one to set them right from all the lies that drive the Red Kingdom into folly and war. They will become victims of this place like so many before them." She pulled her arms through the cloak and fasted the copper tog-gles.

"I did not know it was so bad here," Charlie admitted as she brushed past him toward the door and twisted back the lock.

"This is the most vile place in all of Winter. And it's a shame, really. We used to write ballads and poems about love, not war." Cora opened the door. "Come, Green. I will march you out of the palace as you wish."

FIFTHLY

Trying to keep up with Cora Thimble proved difficult, as she was light on her feet and drifted by palace dwellers with grace. No one questioned where she was going.

Charlie, however, walked very much like he had something to hide.

His boots clanked over the tiles in an unrhythmic beat, drawing suspicious eyes to the weight of his footwear that was made to trek through the wooded arenas and crush sharp, uneven ice in his forest-side village. It was a brutal contrast to the thin black leathers hugging the Red men's calves, and the fabric slipper fashions of the ladies.

Finally, Cora could not seem to take it any longer.

"Did your parents never teach you to walk?" she lectured, casting him a pointed look with her glittering silvers the moment all other beings were out of earshot.

"Not on a floor like *this*," Charlie said, frowning down at it.

Cora's skin tightened as she clutched a brass handle and

swung wide the gemstone doors at the end of the hall. The precious rock tricked Charlie into thinking the doors were heavy, but when he reached to help, Cora slapped his hand away as though insulted.

Charlie decided he would not help her again after that.

A gold entranceway arched at the far end of the long room, and a red carpet stretched down the middle like the one Charlie had seen when he first arrived. Delicate white patterns wove through the rug like crisping snowflakes, and above it, metal cages lined the walls of the room on either side.

The sight brought him to a halt.

The cages were not simply for artifacts or treasures palace dwellers might gaze upon. Inside them were *people*.

Green people.

"Green!" Cora hissed back at him.

But Charlie could not fathom the sight before him: men in Evergreen Host uniforms, others in simple animal skins and olive village attire, put on display like trophies. Were these prisoners of the battles at the borderline?

It did not matter. They were Green. They were his people.

"I cannot leave them here," Charlie apologized as he headed to the nearest cage.

A prisoner looked up when he approached the bars. The man—a huntsman from the looks of him—glanced down at Charlie's red vest.

"Charlie!" Cora used his name this time, her whisper too loud now to conceal from the others passing by in the lobby.

Slipping his hand through the cage, Charlie rested it upon the man's knee which was arched from the way he sat cross-legged in the small space.

"I will get you out of here," Charlie promised.

"No, you won't!" Cora's grip came around Charlie's wrist and she dragged his hand out of the cage. She stole a look back at the lobby. "You're not a hero, Charlie Little. You're not here to save these people!" she added.

"Maybe I am," he challenged, returning her edged stare.

Cora withdrew. She had not seen a look like that upon him thus far. But Charlie could not help it—the beating of his heart had tripped, the sounds around him turned to a jumble—the gossiping people, the giggling whispers, the squeaking of the hinges where the entrance doors opened and shut, the tapping of red slippers over clean tiles...

Charlie winced as a sharp bell thundered through his head. He grabbed his ears, expelling tears from his squeezed eyes.

The ache slithered from his head through the rest of his body like a spear and only evaporated when Cora's hand found his shoulder.

Charlie's white-knuckled fingers still gripped the huntsman's cage. He blinked away the moisture and looked over at her: at Cora Thimble—the Red Kingdom noble who had been handed a comfortable life in the royal Red Kingdom palace, unlike these Greens in cages.

"We need to disappear now, Charlie!" Her fingers tightened around the fabric of his rolled shirt, and she dragged him toward the door.

Charlie took one last look at the caged huntsman before following her out.

33

The glistening black streets of the Scarlet City—the Red Kingdom's glorified capitol—bustled heavier than Charlie might have imagined. Even the most populated regions of the Green Kingdom were sprinkled with forest, so such a measure of people could never have come together in one space.

Flocks of dwellers in fine coats and plush crimson hats slipped around marble legs hoisting crescent towers into the sky. An army of carved gemstone statues watched him from both sides of the road as he passed, and Charlie shuddered.

Sunlight crawled from behind its mask of cloud, turning the statues to prisms of scarlet fire and scattering triangles of red light over the street.

The first time Charlie had heard of a Greed, he had only been six seasons old. According to their neighbours, a Greed had outrun a division of the Evergreen Host on foot, right past Bellbun, appearing as a mere ghost in the forest.

Dozens of the pure white beings wandered the avenues here. *Hundreds*, even—Charlie could not look anywhere without spotting a Greed.

The distractions were overwhelming. Charlie's eyes could not settle; shiny stones speckled every surface, satin garlands wrung pillars, gold sleighs were hauled by dreadfully muscled reindeer, and mist billowed at the end of every street, transforming into mesmerizing shapes against the heavens as it rose.

The multitude of ringing bells was a deafening sound—more clanging of metal than a song. Bronze chimes hung off boots, clothes, and reindeer, pressing a constant clamour into the air that Charlie could not seem to listen past.

"Why do you keep blinking like that?" Cora asked, her feminine voice the only melody amidst the commotion.

"Like what?" But as he asked the question, Charlie realized his lashes were, in fact, fluttering.

"As though your head is splitting into two parts," she returned, pulling an embellished key from her pocket. Her gray eyes fastened to him as she lifted it to a lock.

They had arrived at a wooden door, whittled at the edges and scraped in a spot or three. It blended into the cavern between two white-stone buildings, tucked carefully beneath the shadows, not drawing attention.

"It's all this noise. How can you concentrate?" Charlie rubbed his temples, willing the *clanks* and *clinks* away. Cora only gave him an odd look in response.

She twisted the key against the lock until it clicked—a rusty mechanical sound—then tried the handle.

"Where have you taken me, Red?" Only now did it occur to Charlie that she had led him somewhere, and not just ushered him back to the forest so he could sneak back into the Green Kingdom. He wondered if she doubted his ability to traverse the forest, to hunt for meat, build a fire, and survive in the woods. It was a measure insulting to a Green Kingdom citizen to assume one's incapability in the woods, but perhaps she did not know that.

"We're at a tunnel, Green. A tunnel that is my responsibility to guard." She looked directly into his face now so he would not miss her words. "Not a soul can know I put you in here."

Cora tugged the door, and a screeching sound lifted from where it resisted over a rock floor, only cracking open an inch. Charlie reached to aid her but withdrew when he remembered that she did not like to be helped.

Cora heaved the lumber flap open and leaned her back against it to catch her breath. With a door so uninviting, Charlie wondered if this tunnel had ever been used.

"Your responsibility?" He took a swift look at her, curious as to why she was granted a job as such a young sputtlepun, and a noble one, at that. She couldn't have seen more than ten plus eight seasons. She was also slim and elegant and fragile and as delicate as glass—certainly not the stuff of a guard.

"It was granted to me two seasons ago, plus a quarter, when I reached my ten plus fifth complete season of age."

Charlie added her seasons quickly. She was ten plus seven seasons old, then, and one quarter.

"My father was a keymaker before he passed. It's why I was granted the responsibility to keep *this* key at my hip at all times—" Cora held it up to show him the old iron piece—as long as her hand and certainly heavier, "—so that no citizen can access this hidden passage. And so the Crimson Court will know who to blame if someone ever does." Her stare narrowed.

"I will not speak of it to anyone," Charlie swore, peering into the dark space of dust and cottony cobwebs.

"You'd better not, Charlie Little." She slid the key back into her pocket. "This passage will take you all the way to the gate of the Red Kingdom. You'll be a skip and a hop from the entrance," she said. "Be as invisible as a calling-wicket when you come out the other end, or I will lose my job. Or…" she paused, "something much worse."

"It seems you're quite important," Charlie realized as he

inched into the gloomy space, unsure if he trusted it. The smell of damp earth filled his nostrils.

"Carrying a key is not a difficult job. And people would not suspect me to have it—only five members of the court even know about it. Besides, it will not be my responsibility for much longer." She glanced at the polished wall when she said it, a dreary look screening her gray eyes to chalky stones. It brought Charlie's attention back.

"You'll get a new assignment?" he guessed.

"It's a long tale," she said. "As soon as one of the Directors of Tournaments announces their retirement, I know they will come for me next to fill the role. They have not kept it a secret."

Beneath her pale fingers, she gripped the iron handle of the door where she leaned for more support than she might have realized.

"I'll admit, I don't know what that is." Charlie folded his arms, content to stay with her a pinch longer instead of facing the gloomy tunnel. But when her stare returned, there was recognition in her cloudy eyes.

"I've already said too much. You're not supposed to know things about us, Green."

"I think it's too late for that." Charlie chuckled, thinking of how much of the palace he had already mapped out in his mind, the numbers he had counted in the streets, and this secret passage he now knew of that tunnelled right into the heart of the Scarlet City. It would be Cora's demise, but Charlie was sure he could bring all this information to the King of the Pines in exchange for his freedom. In fact, such information might give the Evergreen Host enough of an advantage to sneak into the capitol, infiltrate the palace, and win the war. The King of the Pines would have no use for Charlie, or his talents, after that.

But Charlie would not do that to Cora Thimble.

"Well, if you must know, a Director of Tournaments is someone who oversees the cruelest aspects of the Red Kingdom's entertainment," she said, gripping her arms to herself. "And I could do it well because I'm creative. But I am not twisted like the directors of the past. I don't wish to be in charge of prisoners, or to assign punishments for our enemies. But my mother offered me for the assignment because I'm..." Cora's concentration hovered in the air, her eyes resting on Charlie for a moment before darting to the alley they had come through, her cheeks like blooming red roses.

"You are what?" Truly, Charlie could not fathom Cora being forced into such a role. She was glass and sugar and moondust. How terrible it would be for someone like that to make cruel decisions such as those. But her story left him on edge, and he pressed his weight against his toes, leaning in to hear what she would say.

It seemed she could not say it.

Cora's mouth was shut when she drew her stare back. More than once thus far she had reminded Charlie that she did not trust him. It seemed that had not changed even though she had spared him from getting captured by the palace guards.

"Because I'm pleasant to look at."

When she finally said it, Charlie tilted back onto his heels. He was the one who could not speak now.

Cora's mother was not wrong. Cora was graced with features that ought to be looked at, the sort that might draw attention to her even when she did not want it. Since the moment Charlie had met her, he had seen silver fires flickering behind her lovely eyes.

But he had not expected it to be something the royal Reds would take advantage of.

"Just go, Green." She only whispered now. Her once-hard stare could not seem to meet his eyes.

"I will." Charlie slid into the tunnel. "But perhaps you are best off to come with me after all," he said for the second time now, meaning it more this time than the last.

There it was again—that same smirk that stole her berry-glossed lips as before when he had suggested the idea. Not mockery: it was more of an indication that he did not understand the situation in full.

"Goodbye, Green. Do not stop for anyone at the gate. Keep moving until you are far away from this kingdom. And if you're wise, you'll never come back here."

SIXTHLY

The tunnel was worse than Charlie expected; no windows or cracks in the walls to allow a thread of light in to help him find his way. He was forced to pat the chilled stones at his sides and drag his feet slowly over the floor to keep himself from stumbling.

He should have been pondering his escape—planning how he might run for the Red Kingdom gate when he spotted light again. Pondering getting back to Green and finding his parents who would be ill with fret. He would have been wise to fixate on ideas to spin the King of the Pines off his trail, and to free himself from a forthcoming life of service to the Evergreen Host.

But all Charlie could think about was what Cora Thimble had said.

The passage was tranquil, the smashing of bells having melted behind him at the tunnel entrance. It was a welcome relief for his ears.

He replayed the moment in the palace lobby when a mind-splitting shriek had nearly burst his ears open, a thing no other soul had cringed at. He'd never felt a thing invade his body in such a way. But the moment Cora's hand had taken his shoulder, the pain had fizzled away like steam.

"Perhaps she has a gift, too? Though I doubt she knows it." Charlie guessed aloud into the blank space of soggy stones. He was certain Elowin could hear him, as he guessed that Elowin had always heard his songs, perhaps even joined in them once or twice.

But all was quiet in the tunnel.

A rocky bend acted as a black curtain. As Charlie rounded it, spotted streams of light leaking into the passage ahead. His feet scurried towards freedom—his boots packed with dense mud now, twice as weighty as when he began.

Sunlight boxed the shadow of a door and Charlie bowed back at the hollow tunnel to bid it farewell. He trotted up a set of rubble-coated stairs and pushed through the door into the chilly floral and spice-scented air.

The piercing blue of the sky nipped at his eyes, and he lifted a hand to shield his face. A steady hum deluged his ears, a bass note that forbade Charlie to use it as fuel, for it was not a product of something beautiful. No, this was a tenor that seeped from a dark corner or valley, or something hidden deep below the ground.

It brought Charlie's feet together at the street's edge and thwarted his notice of the individuals passing him by. For a measure, Charlie stared at nothing at all, trying to isolate the noise that overwhelmed his skin with prickles. The peculiar symphony was not familiar, and *pinespittle*, he did not like it.

"That's him!" A cry lifted Charlie from his stupor.

A man in the street wore a familiar crimson garment, but it wasn't just any Ruby Legionnaire. It was the very brute Charlie had met as he tumbled onto the red carpet when he had first arrived.

This guard knew Charlie's face. He had seen him wearing green.

He must have come to watch for him at the Red Kingdom gate.

Charlie sprang behind a wagon and twisted behind cherry banners with noble identification symbols being raised.

Red paint coated the eyelids of a sled-driver who stood at the sight of Charlie's fumbling. "Watch your scotcher, boy!" he snapped.

It was loud enough to aim the search of the palace guards that had flitted into the street at the first guard's shouting.

Charlie turned for a new direction but found only a broad chest embossed with fine gold threads, a crimson cape hugging wide shoulders, and bronze buttons down a clean ivory shirt.

There was not time for Charlie to spring back before the Ruby soldier snatched his arms, allowing the remaining palace guards to reach them.

"Wait!" Charlie tried. Ideas sparked in his mind—ones of talking his way out or yanking away with enough jolt to free himself. Of singing, maybe.

But the guards did not seem interested in his plea. Charlie's hands were secured together with a tight wire.

"Please," Charlie tried again, finding the palace guard who had recognized him—a stout man with a snarl thinning his mouth and hard glass eyes. "I'm not what you think. I stumbled into your palace on accident. I'm not a spy."

"Quiet, sputtlepun. We'll know your secrets soon enough."

Charlie tripped into an uneven walk as the guards edged him with their elbows and spears. Citizens halted their hobbies to gaze upon him, absorbing the features of the enemy Green.

If only Charlie could clarify that he did not represent the King of the Pines or the Evergreen Host. Charlie opened his mouth to enlighten the guards, but before a word flitted off his tongue, a hilt knocked the back of his head, and he crumpled into a snowdrift. All the crimsons and cherries and flags and floats, the eerie music, and the trotting reindeer slipped away to leave a precious quiet in his spinning mind.

Sounds of displeased grunts awoke him. Charlie's hands were still bound. The vest he had taken from the costume room had been cut off, leaving him with only his stretched tunic and rolled up sleeves. The throbbing in his head might have drummed the rhythm of a dreadful song if there was any other music to be heard, but apart from the grumbles of the people standing in a tight line beside him, all was quiet in this narrow room.

Dim lights saturated the space with colourless hues, and everything smelled of sweat and hopelessness. The hot, sticky temperature was drastically different than what it had been outside. Charlie felt heavy; his mind was not quite right. Dizziness pulled him forward and backward in a teeter.

A light blinked to life in an adjacent room, separated from those in Charlie's line by only a wall of handprinted glass. On the other side, people stood in fine garments—some with crowns.

The thought awoke his senses, bringing him to stand upright. A man in the middle had a thick velvet cape sprinkled with precious ruby flakes. The polished crown upon his head said everything.

The Crimson King. The man Charlie had heard so many terrible stories about.

The king was much younger than Charlie expected, perhaps only ten full seasons more accomplished in his timestring than Charlie himself.

Only now did Charlie pay attention to where he was and try to guess what this was about. Beside him, the other men were also restrained with wiry binds. They all sweated together as equals, staring ahead at those beyond the wall of glass whom Charlie guessed would decide their fate.

Charlie's stare moved over royals and nobles, his blinking attention stopping on one individual hovering off to the side. Her hair was already fashioned differently than when he had left, and a neutral look was crafted onto her fair face.

Cora Thimble did not look pleased to see him there. In fact, she did not take a single look at any of the other prisoners in Charlie's room. Flashes of accusation danced through the sharp gray of her eyes as she stared at Charlie and Charlie alone.

He wondered if he had gotten her in trouble. Cora had been clear about not getting caught by the tunnel exit. Did the Reds know that she had allowed him to pass through the secret passageway? Would she be reprimanded, or worse?

But by the way the nobles did not cast a glance in Cora's direction, Charlie thought that maybe no one knew yet what Cora had done. Perhaps they had not pieced together how Charlie had been able to sneak to the Red Kingdom gate so fast, or how he had managed to escape from the palace in the first place.

Charlie pulled his gaze down to the damp floor so he would not give Cora away. What would the dreaded Crimson King think if he saw one of the prisoners sharing looks with someone of his noble court?

A young royal who could not be more than six seasons old lifted his hand and pointed to one of the men in Charlie's room. From the corner of his eye, Charlie thought he noticed a sigh of relief deflate Cora's chest. But the next little boy, even younger than the first, with a thin crown of twisted metals upon his ivory hair, lifted his hand, and Charlie felt his heart falter as the aim of the toddler's finger could not be mistaken. He pointed directly at Charlie.

Charlie glanced back at Cora to find her eyes closed, her sugared lips pursed, and a shadow of a crease between her brows.

There was no telling what Charlie had been chosen for, or why. But Charlie knew the rumours of the Red royals. He knew he had been selected for something dreadful. Something that even the strong-faced Cora Thimble could not look upon him for.

SEVENTHLY

Orange from the evening sunset burned through the stained-glass windows, twisting the natural scarlet petals to fiery, sour clementine leaves. Though the luminosity burned his eyes, Charlie could not look away from the glass that pillared the curved wall of the spacious dining hall, or the flecks of scattered flames prismed around the room where the sun leaked its colours.

Red and gold runners blanketed a mahogany table set for thirty plus six. Sculptures of ice dripped casually in the table's centre, elegant artwork of twists and spirals, some mimicking people or birds or rare flowers. Surrounding them were copper platters of tall cakes and sweets sprinkled with sparkling sugar-powder and oval glass bowls that were filled to the brim with dark chocolates and cream pudding cups.

It was all rather delicate and dramatic. Certainly not how

Greens feasted—dropping onto wood-chiselled chairs and biting into fire roasted meat with their teeth whilst drums beat rhythms into the forest to chase away hungry birds. The Reds were not as hungry as the Greens, it seemed.

Charlie tugged on the bindings at his wrists, finding them just as stubborn as the last time he tried. He was certain he would not be able to run out of the palace on his own anyway, should his bindings suddenly split apart and fall.

He sighed, scanning the scruffy lad beside him whose pale mane of hair was split into sections and braided, giving him exactly four long tails down his back. The young man tried to keep his head high, but Charlie spotted the shuffling of his feet and the waters pooling at the corners of his eyes.

"You seem to know why we're here," Charlie whispered as the royal family entered with a gaudy blast of trumpets to spoil the serenity of the room.

The lad's periwinkle eyes darted to Charlie with a touch of accusation. "Do not speak, boy, or they will make our punishment far worse."

At that, Charlie left the lad alone, searching instead for Cora who drifted in at the back of the flock of nobles in shimmering feathers, hiding their wicked talons beneath stretchy hose and fluffy skirts. She was in a rosebud sash with sparkling apple-toned jewels scattered into the layers of her skirts.

Cora found him immediately. Her bunched brows were as solid as the marble posts she passed, her moonbeam eyes travelling over him in a quick search. A search for what though? He couldn't guess. Perhaps she wished to know he wasn't hurt.

He tried not to feel elated, but a smile may have dented

his cheek, even with his mysterious punishment creeping up on him.

The nobles waited for the Crimson King to take his seat at the head of the table, where a throne of gold and cherry velvet invited him. Charlie tried not to roll his eyes as the king sat. The act permitted the rest of the guests to sit, too.

"Let us dedicate these moments to the oaths of our kingdom, and to our prophets who keep us aligned with the stars." The Crimson King's voice was airy and rusty, as though his throat was swelled. There was no sweetness or musical note to be heard.

The room erupted with a chant of voices reciting a ballad. *"May the Red paint spread, and bring the globe to order, as our prophets lead the way with visions and treasured script."*

Charlie swallowed a grunt. He had felt true magic and power in songs—the authentic music of the snow which these Reds stifled with gongs and bells and smoke and chimes. This company knew nothing of honest order, true visions, or treasures.

He thought of Elowin roaming the serene channels of the hidden library, tucked away in peace.

"Entertain us!" The Crimson King's shout made the lad beside Charlie jump. "You first, thief! And give us your best, as the prisoner who entertains me the least will be tossed into the arena."

This time when Charlie glanced at the lad with braids, he did so with rounded eyes, for he only now realized what sort of competition this was.

The lad's throat bobbed, but he nodded and raised his bound wrists. "I'll need these off to entertain you, my King."

"Yes. Miss Thimble, free the man!" The king waved a copper spoon through the air and Charlie's stare shot to Cora, who paled. But she rose, modestly and without a ruckus, her snowy skirts twinkling by the dimming sunset, and drew a silver key from a hidden pocket of her dress. She kept her eyelids down as she approached, a blush leaking into her cheeks like the sweetest berry juice. With a quick twist, she dropped the lock binding the cord at the lad's wrists and stole one flickering glance at Charlie. Her eyes were swimming gray clouds.

"I hope you win," she whispered to him. "But I cannot help you if you don't."

It was the only thing she said before showing Charlie the laced-up back of her dress and gliding back to her chair. Charlie bit his lips together. Cora Thimble was special, indeed. She was being watched, more so than she had let on. He bristled at the thought of this king preparing her to be a ruthless Director of Tournaments.

The lad beside Charlie slid into a low bow. The clinking of rings being passed around filled the table as the nobles and royal family placed their bets on the prisoners with giggles and banter. Fresh courses were carried out by elves from a steaming hallway, all with matching claret ribbons winding their limbs. Fizzing drinks sloshed in wide glass goblets as they were lifted to tulip-red lips around the table.

When the lad with braids lifted from his bow, he raised a graceful arm, nearly swatting Charlie away with it. Nobles whistled and raised their goblets with chuckles. The prisoner's braids flapped as he lifted to his tiptoes and spun, waving his dirt-smudged fingers in the air. But it wasn't graceful. It seemed this lad might not have really been a dancer, even though he was trying to prove he was one.

Charlie watched the whole unusual performance, even as the nobles' banter died to silence, some grimacing through their chewing. They studied the prancing prisoner until one of the royal sons slid from his chair, snatched a vase off a nearby bench, and ran around the table with it.

Snickers amplified when the ivory-haired boy thrust the vase toward the prisoner and a thick river of bloodred paint splashed up the side of his face. Then it was clanging cymbals of laughter. The prisoner stifled a shudder, but continued on, his speckled-red face contorting as he lunged through the silence where not a drip of music aided his performance. He was simply a man dancing to nothing, for people who mocked him for it.

So, this was the competition, then. Not really a contest at all, but a chance for the king and his accomplices to ridicule to their hearts' content while cranberry sauce dripped from their chins and their tongues licked the remains of sugar off their cutlery.

Suddenly, the prisoner swung himself towards the dining room doors. The lad's braids slapped around his body as he sprinted on light-padded soles into the hallway where Charlie could no longer see.

"Fetch him!" the Crimson King snarled with a new laugh escaping his throat, and six Ruby Legion guards drew their weapons to end the escape attempt, gliding from the feast with their silken capes brushing the air.

"You should catch him yourself, Your Majesty. It would be good practice for chasing the King of the Pines in the Silver Jubilee Renewal in the quarter next." A lady with pear-shaped diamond earrings shot the king a smile, drawing new chuckles from the nobles.

"Ha! I'll practice another day, perhaps." The Crimson King's gaze shot to Charlie, who froze. "Your turn. Impress us, spy!"

Cora's eyes were closed now, sealing away their moon-dust colours. It seemed she was not breathing.

Though he was certain he would be blasted with paint as the first prisoner had been, Charlie cleared his throat. He did not have many skills to be proud of, but he did have one. One he hoped might spare him the dreadful arena of the Scarlet City.

Hearing any sort of reliable song over the spritzing drinks and clamouring cutlery was a chore, but Charlie split through the unpleasant sounds, placing them aside to find a thread of true music that might be whispering amidst it all. He exhaled a sweet note, letting it slide out easily into the room.

Beyond the table were the windows, and beyond those, the sun, speaking its last message of warmth before it might disappear and the stars would watch in its place. There was not much of a breeze, but Charlie imagined it out there, sing-ing skyward above the buildings where it could not be in-fected by the clatter of the Reds. He sang an old tune—one he had sung just a few times before to chase off chills in the air. It rose from the snow, descended from the sky, moved in with the wind.

"Quiet, can you hear the song?
Creation has been singing it all along,
For, it knows who painted its colours,
It knows who painted its colours.

Listen, can you hear the sound?
Look skyward, where the sun abounds,
Let creation sing of its colours,
Let creation sing of its colours."

Charlie's heart, which had been suffering in its rhythms, slowed to its natural pace as his body clung to the melody and was restored by it.

When he looked out at the glassy table, he realized the room was quiet. Much *too* quiet, in fact—a sea of people as still and silent as the ice sculptures in their midst. His eyes shot to Cora Thimble, who was standing at her place by the table. Her wide eyes were brimmed with moisture; an escaped bead clung to her cheek. She seemed to realize it and shuffled back down to her seat, brushing the tear away with the back of her hand, a wave of her hair falling to hide the look on her face.

The Crimson King rose in a slow, calculated manner, his crown glittering atop his dark locks of hair. "I can think of a way or three to use you, boy," he said.

Charlie's face fell, the unrhythmic pulsing of his heart returning. He wondered if this really had been part of Elowin's plan, as Cora had guessed. But it did not make a pinch of sense for Elowin to have rescued Charlie from the King of the Pines only to have the Crimson King use him instead.

EIGHTLY

Charlie was thrust into a cage in the lobby with the other *decorations*. He found himself in a black-barred encompassment too small for his legs to straighten.

As they left, the Ruby Legion guards studied him differently than how they had looked upon him before.

The palace lobby was dim at this late hour. Muffled snores lifted from distant cages stationed too far away for Charlie to converse with their inhabitants naturally. He decided to let his fellow cage-men sleep and ask them plenty of questions when dawn arrived.

But he did not make it to dawn.

In the midnight stillness, beneath a navy sky of diamond stars only seen through the nearest window, someone arrived in a white hooded cloak. Her light hair glowed even beneath the blueish nighttime haze.

She came to the cage and stood an inch from the bars,

revealing her silver-blade eyes. Cora's skin was bleached white from the direct moonlight.

"You will get yourself into trouble if you're caught," Charlie reminded her.

Cora stared at him, seeming unburdened by his warning. "I know what you're here for, Charlie Little," she said, and Charlie shrunk down to sit on his knees.

"What do you mean?"

"I've figured out who Elowin is and why he did this." Her fingers came around the smooth black bars, showing a delicate copper ring on her forefinger.

Charlie took hold of the bars between them, just below her hands, lowering so his face was not far from hers. He kept his voice down. "Tell me what you've discovered, Red."

"There is a girl who sings spells and moves to take dominion over territories, not truly for the King of the Pines, but for a master much worse. She's a breathing lie," Cora said. "You are her opposition."

Charlie drew back a measure. "You mean Melody Carol? That little girl of the Evergreen Host?"

"You know of her?" Cora's face changed.

"I do. I've seen her. I..." As the memory trickled in, Charlie recalled how his song had settled the storm and realized it was exactly as Cora said. "I stopped her storm. I sang back in Bellbun when she tried to drown my street in a current of snow. Her spell evaporated."

White leaked into Cora's knuckles as her grip tightened on the poles.

Yes, he and Melody Carol were perhaps two ends of the same string.

"Elowin is the ancient Truth I've met in my dreams. He is the True King of Winter the old prophets spoke of. His voice is the living Truth itself." She paused. "You have Elowin's voice within you, Charlie. Your praise sends the darkness fleeing. The girl you crossed carries one of the many voices of the giant—the *Beast*. But you, Charlie, you're meant to quiet the noise. You're meant to help me assemble the secret cathedral in Room Four Hundred Plus Six."

Charlie released his grip and raised his hands to pause the lovely rant. "Miss Thimble, you're speaking of things I've never heard of," he admitted. "I don't even know what a secret cathedral is."

"I'll tell you, but first *listen*. The Red Kingdom is full of noise, Charlie. Can't you hear it?" A glisten sparkled in the corner of her eye against the moonglow, much like the tear that had sprouted when she first heard him sing in the dining hall. "I didn't know how I was to reach people through all of the *noise* and the *lies*. But you can reach them. You can quiet a room; I just saw it."

Charlie faltered when she slid a key from her pocket, a dark brass piece with a flat oval handle. "What are you doing?"

"I'm getting you out of this cage. If you must, you can go home. But I want you to come back." A *click* filled the quiet lobby when she slid the key into the mechanism. The lock fell free, clattering over the floor and making the other prisoners stir.

Charlie looked out at his fellow Greens, bound by dark bars and tiny spaces. He would free them soon; he was certain of it.

"I can't go home." Charlie's face fell as he admitted it. The cage door squeaked open. "The Evergreen Host is looking for me. For my gift." He paused, then hopped out of the cell, landing quieter than the squawking cage door had been. "But I must send a message to my parents."

Cora's shoulders relaxed and a lovely smile stole her mouth, possibly the sincerest one Charlie had witnessed since they met. "Well, then. I'll hide you in a room outside the Scarlet City that I once saw in a dream."

Her hand came out to shake his.

Charlie stared at it for a measure, then took it. Her skin was soft, and he felt the press of her rings against his fingers.

"Welcome to the underground church, Charlie Little."

NINTHLY

Cora pulled a garment from beneath her own cape as they rushed from the lobby and into the chill-kissed night.

At first, Charlie scowled at the rolled cloak. "It's *red*," he complained, but one pointed look from Cora told him he would put it on or be left behind to test the Ruby Legion guards on his own. Before they reached the ice bridge, the cloak was on his shoulders.

They strode through an orchard of pure-white apples, through a garden of ice sculptures glistening beneath the twinkling stars above, and beneath the cover of a wall of crimson pines.

Past all that lay a quiet city, and in this city was an inn of antique iron and glass, and in this inn was an Inn Keeper whose smile, Charlie realized, was made of the sun itself; pure and free and ready for the future. The Inn Keeper handed Cora a new key for her collection, one with a ticket dangling from it that read: ROOM 406.

There was no Room Four Hundred Plus Six in the main hallways, but Cora and Charlie searched through the late hours of the night until they came back to the blooming water fountain outside.

Charlie was a pinch away from giving up when he spotted the old door on the Inn's hip; chipping wood, faded paint, and rusted hinges. A dull gold plate hung tilted on the door's face with a number barely legible.

"By the sharpest wind, there it is…" Cora breathed when she followed his stare.

"Not much to look at," Charlie commented. It was a door certainly concealed by its own unattractiveness.

But the key fit. Cora turned it, and the door unlocked, opening with a silent sweep. "We're here," she whispered. "Charlie…this is it. This is the place from my dreams. Truly, I didn't know if it was real until this moment."

Charlie followed her in, eyeing the dark corners as Cora moved to a table and fiddled with a match and lantern. Once she had it lit, the angular walls and ceiling of the room—or *rooms*—appeared to be much too large to be so unnoticed by the guests who travelled through the inn. It was as though the space did not truly exist until one stepped inside it.

Charlie took in a deep breath, feeling that this moment was one he would remember right to the final breaths on his timestring, though he did not yet grasp why.

"I see you made it." That familiar voice of springs and sunrises filled the dim air with the sweet light of harmonies.

When Charlie turned, he blinked at the being who stood there—the one Cora had described as having the voice of Truth itself.

"Did you think we wouldn't make it?" Charlie asked,

fighting a silly smile.

Elowin smiled, too. "Many before you didn't."

Charlie's face fell at that.

"What is our assignment, Elowin? Why have you been showing me dreams of a network of hope in the shadows?" Cora appeared at Charlie's side like a loyal partner, a gesture Charlie did not mind at all.

"I believe you already possess the answer to that question. You're to start the underground cathedral, Cora Thimble."

Cora exhaled. "So, it's true."

"But why?" Charlie asked.

"Because a time is coming soon when an ancient enemy will rise. For a short measure, I will show myself to the kingdoms and some will remember me as their king, the one who formed the snow beneath their boots. And in these coming days, I will raise up a generation of bold young ones who will carry the sacred truths into the corners of the globe. But then I will be taken and killed by this great ancient enemy who will defile the nations with darkness and lies, twisting the old ways this way and that. And the strength of the believers will collapse."

Charlie felt Cora's dainty fingers slide into his, gripping his hand as she listened.

"What will become of the cathedral then?" Charlie asked.

"Your numbers will suffer at the enemy's deception. But stay steadfast in my plan, and you'll establish shields on your souls," Elowin said, his rainbow eyes a glowing artwork in the dark. "Until then, build this cathedral. Scribe hymnals and aid the orphans and widows in the streets."

"How should we build this house of believers?" Cora's

voice was not quiet or frightened, and for that, Charlie admired her a pinch more.

The lantern's flame sizzled quietly from its table, a gentle hum to mirror the inner flames sparking inside those in Room Four Hundred Plus Six.

"Like this," Elowin said. "Go into the Winter world and speak the truths. In the springs, baptize those who would join you in my name, and in the name of the Truth. Teach them the Wisdom. And know that I am with you always, to the end of this age, even in the quarters when the skies grow dark, and after the morning my blood is spilled into the snow."

"You'll be dead?" Charlie objected; certain this plan was crazy.

But a slight smile found the mouth of the one Cora had called the Truth itself. "Do not be afraid, Charlie Little. We never truly die." A warm wind moved through Room Four Hundred Plus Six. And Elowin's eyes twinkled when he said, "I will come back."

LASTLY, AND SO FORTH

It went this way for many full seasons. Charlie Little aided Cora Thimble in her fight; they rallied the servants and nobles, the citizens and messengers, the bronzesmiths and glassworkers, the actresses and the chocolatiers. A legendary pair they made—a songbird to crack open the darkest veils shadowing the eyes of the blind, and a keymaker's apprentice giving him access to every wicked corner, whilst giving those in need entrance to the cathedral in Room Four Hundred Plus Six. A mysterious room, it was. One with brittle boards, foggy windows, and rusted hinges, just past the silver fountain and tucked below a quiet inn.

The hidden church of Elowin flourished by their work, and the Truth spread, until their numbers stretched across the Red Kingdom, hiding in the crevices of every great monument and edifice, slipping amidst the throngs of each spectacle and event, whispering their choruses into withered piles of dead bones to see them rise and dance once again.

The legends of Charlie Little and Cora Thimble would not perish, even in the late seasons of their timestrings. Even when a darkness would rise from the kingdom floors in retaliation and demonstrate awe-inspiring evils to strike back. Even when a great and terrible Beast of the Night might show himself in the end.

A time would come when all that was good and true would be attacked, every soul would be tested, every thought of belief would be challenged by backwards rationality.

But the message is simple—one penned by Cora Thimble herself in the late seasons of her timestring:

Dear Church,

Do not fear the Beast.
He is the lesser of the two who will duel in the end.

-C.T.

THE

FOUNTAIN

OF

WISHES

Novella, The Second

Once upon a Winter's snow
A Prince of Green felt quite alone
He wished on a fountain with a modest prayer
To see just how his fate would fare...

FIRSTLY

It was an unofficial crime in the Green Kingdom to *not* hoot and holler and shriek and fuss at the feasts. Edward Green knew as much, yet he often could not find himself lured in by the sweet call of sugary nectar drizzled over hot roasted bird, or the cooked citrus slices spread evenly over the sizzling forest boar. The fermented ciders did not entertain him, and the heaps of smoked sausages dunked in olive butters did not get a second glance from the young prince, either. He was not the quiet sort, but he was *certainly* not the loud sort. He was somewhere in between the two, with no place of his own.

The spoon between his fingers was as cold as the frost on the grassy floor where the royal family dined at the long lumber table with seats for everyone in his father's council. The place settings stretched further into the forest than he could see, and Edward often wondered how long it took the servants of Timber Castle to prepare such large feasts at every sunrise and sunset, and how they kept the birds from swooping in to eat it all before the guests arrived.

The king was a large man, as muscled as any Green huntsman. A large, loud man.

Edward could only wince when his father's dark beard dipped into the steaming berry soup with his every bite. He was a king praised by the inner woods cities but hated by the villagers beyond. Though, in the king's defense, the man hadn't a clue how the villages felt about things.

But Edward did.

Across the table, Edward's sister laughed at the gory stories—ones of hunting and slaying large animals, of tracking the snowsquatches, and of the iron-clashing war on their kingdom's brink that never slept. Ever Green was not shy or unsure like Edward; she kept her chin high and her eyes bright, her laugh loud and her skin thick. She was a season plus two quarters younger than he, but in many ways, she was beyond his seasons in matters of leadership.

Ever was the one the King of the Pines called upon to hunt with him. The king had not called upon his son and heir since Edward once refused to learn how traps were set, how animals were skinned, and how fires blazed to cook the meat. It was not that he didn't care, rather, he just had other things on his mind.

Edward Green had another life he wished for and another name he had given himself. He had a distant village he had called his home a time or three, where he would sneak in to toss a ball with the other young boys and never admit to them who he was.

The terrible secret was that Edward knew how to be ordinary. He knew how to be hungry, unlike those who feasted at his father's table. But often, he was reminded that he did not know how to be extraordinary. Like a king.

"To the King of the Pines! May his victory in the Silver Jubilee Renewal at tomorrow's midday change the course of the war!" one of the generals shouted, his wooden armour clapping at his elbows.

At the gesture, fifty soldiers plus five raised their glasses of fermented cider and cheered for the king, who bellowed a laugh and raised his own glass to himself, too. Cups were smashed down the table, bits of glass or clay spilling away from the tabletop into the grassy forest carpet. All were so certain their king would still be alive after tomorrow.

Edward twisted in his seat, his eyes flickering past the gingerbread sculptures dotted with mint twists and other sweets, and he found his sister cheering along with the men. What would it do to Ever if the king did not live through the Renewal?

Timber Castle was almost empty when the evening feast finished. Tall, spiral staircases reached up through every level of the palace like ribbons, the hallways carpeted with emerald velvet. It was all unlit—not a candle or fireplace gave off a lick of warmth. Edward marched over the creaking hardwood floors toward his chambers, determined to make it there before anyone else caught up. But he was not as lucky of a boy as most.

"Edward." He halted at the sound of his name but relaxed when he recognized Shanely's light, scratchy tone.

"You missed the feast, Professor. My father probably noticed. You may want to lay low until…" As Edward turned, he could not find the right words to finish the sentence to his education minister.

Until after tomorrow, when my father may no longer be alive, was what he did not say. But it seemed Shanely understood well enough.

The old man's hair was thinning up top, and his kind maize eyes were wrapped with a nest of wrinkles—"*wisdom,*" Shanely had claimed once during their lessons.

Even in the dark, Edward could see Shanely's hands tremble with age as he raised them to his student's shoulders. "We don't know what will happen tomorrow, Edward. We don't know that you'll have to become the King of the Pines."

"It doesn't matter," Edward pointed out. "I'll have to, eventually. My father's timestring won't go on forever, even if he does survive the Crimson King at tomorrow's midday."

Shanely put an arm around the Green Prince and walked with him through the dim halls. "Well then, son, I guess the question now is..." the professor began as he ventured into Edward's chambers and over to the study area. Papers and books were stacked from their most recent lessons.

Edward waited for the man to finish, watching as Shanely lit a lantern that painted the walls with gold.

Finally, Shanely sat down in his instructors' chair and folded his hands atop his lap, even though it was far too late for a lesson and tomorrow was a rather important day. "The question now is, what are you going to do about it?" the man finally asked.

Edward folded his arms, studying the graying professor who had taught him of histories and sciences and art and poetry ever since he was a boy. Most of the other educators found Shanely to be odd, and Edward had never had a difficult time understanding why. But there was a glimmer in

Shanely's eye tonight, and Edward couldn't guess what it was about.

"No riddles tonight, Professor. I'm far too tired."

Shanely sighed. "Not a riddle. Just a question," he corrected.

"Then why do I feel as though this is a test?" Edward unfolded his arms and slid the top book off the nearest pile to scan the cover. "You're always full of tests."

"Not tonight, son."

The way the man said it brought Edward's eyes back up. "Shanely?"

"You don't want to be King," Shanely said, and Edward went still, the book balancing on his fingers. "Come on, Edward. I've been your teacher for ten plus two seasons, since you were old enough to hold an ink pen. That's a long measure to know someone."

Edward set the book down with a great thud. "Are you trying to get me in trouble?"

"I'm *trying* to save your life." The glimmer of jest had left the professor's eyes now, and all that remained were shards of orange worry amidst the maize.

Edward should have fought it, denied it, thrown a fit over such an accusation. But he found himself dropping into the chair across from his professor, a slick coat of moisture filming his eyes. "What do I do?" For a boy who was a rather impeccable actor in the villages when he pretended to be something he was not, his voice trembled.

But Shanely did not seem eager to pounce or accuse. The aged man looked upon his prince, the heir, the one responsibility he had possessed in a great measure of seasons, and he whispered, "Run."

SECONDLY

The night had been dreadful; birds squawked outside the wood shutters, and the darkness had found its voice, tormenting Edward with ballads of wind and silence in between its breaths. His sheets grew itchy, his pillow too hard. Things he had never noticed before.

When the dawn broke loose over the mountains, the young prince rose with the morning—his feet cold, his heart heavy, and his mind pulling him in a multitude of directions. He fastened a cloak over his sleepwear and slipped out of his room unnoticed by the Evergreen Host soldiers at the end of the hall.

From there he made his way to the lowest balcony and hopped off the ledge—a thing he had not done since the early seasons of his timestring. A thing he would not be able to get away with again for a good measure. He slipped through the curtains of garland speckled with twinkling lights and silver bells, and the prince chased the wind through the trees on light feet.

The Silver Jubilee Renewal was rushing in. It would arrive at noon whether Edward was ready for it or not. Two kings would fight until only one lived, and Edward would either be forced to become one of the youngest kings in the history of the Pines, or he would be able to stay a prince for a measure longer.

As he ran, Edward gazed through the threads of snowy trees toward the villages too far away to hear or see, villages he had crept through a time or three in a desperate hope to make friends. He had made some, ones he had kept only by using a false name. But one friend especially had made him laugh harder than he ever had during his seasons in Timber Castle. It was a boy named Charlie Little who sang the storms away. Charlie made Edward believe that fear was only temporary, like the squalls of snow passing through the village.

But Charlie was long gone, a good memory from the past. Edward had run through the night to warn his friend to leave the kingdom the moment news of Charlie's musical gift had reached the Council of Pines. Edward had not tried to find Charlie or visit the Little family again after that.

Edward had watched the Evergreen Host grow harsher in their recruitment over the seasons. He had cringed as they gathered young sputtlepun children with gifts. And he had grown ill with the realization that he would be expected to reign viciously as his father had, taking every measure possible to win the war and crush the Reds. That is, until twenty plus five seasons had passed, and Edward would be forced to battle in the Silver Jubilee Renewal himself against whatever ruler sat upon the Crimson throne. It was a shameful, ridiculous, bloody tradition. And for all his seasons, Edward could not understand why the kingdoms continued to glorify it.

Sweat clung to Edward's neck when he reached the fountain. Patches of ice floated on the ever-rippling waters like ice boats on the snowseas. Shanely had taken Edward for a walk here for the first time when he was only seven seasons old. The old man had called it *the Fountain of Wishes*.

"It used to be called the Fountain of Prayers, you know," Shanely had said at the time. *"Villagers and nobles alike would come to this well and offer prayers to an ancient Truth that our kingdom no longer talks about. Now, the few who still bother to trek here toss in rings in exchange for flimsy wishes that will never come true."*

"Did the prayers used to come true before the name of the fountain was changed?" Edward had asked as he'd climbed onto the fountain's edge and poked a finger into the ice-cold water.

But Shanely had laughed. *"What could you possibly have to pray about, son? You're the Prince of the Pines. You snap your fingers and you have a feast. You clap your hands and music is played."* The older man had paused though. *"But perhaps one day you'll have something to pray about. Perhaps that's why I brought you here."*

The professor had said nothing more about it. But Shanely had always been a man of mysteries and riddles that left Edward guessing.

Edward pulled down the hood of his cloak and watched the blue-black pool swirl in the fountain. Water tumbled from the beak of a white bird statue into the mote. The bird was chipped in so many places, it hardly resembled an animal anymore.

The quiet forest hummed as Edward reached for the ring on his forefinger and slid it off with care. He eyed the silver piece, inlaid with a band of wood. And then he tossed it into the water.

"I'm not religious," he admitted to the fountain, so it would not think him a liar or trickster. "But I'm feeling very alone today." That was all—he did not state his prayers or wishes aloud. He simply watched the water bubble in silence.

The morning skies clouded with gray as heavy air swept in. The day was splitting.

So, the Prince of the Pines turned from the old fountain and walked back to Timber Castle.

"*Edward*!" Ever's voice came from outside his door.

Edward fastened his buckles and tugged his wood armour over his shoulders. "Come in," he said.

His sister's wild, dark braids fell every which way, her silver eyes bright like steel. "There's a snowsquatch outside the castle!" she exclaimed with a curled mouth. "Do you want to watch the Host take it down?"

Edward blinked. "Can't they just let that young, dreadful girl chase it off with her songs?" he asked, but Ever snorted a laugh.

"Melody Carol? She's not dreadful at all. We've become friends." Edward tried not to shudder at the thought of Ever

75

with such a strange, powerful girl. "And besides, the Evergreen Host want to capture it for sport," she went on.

Truly, Edward did not know why Ever had come to invite him. Perhaps it was her way of standing by him when the next measure of hours would determine his fate. He had never been close to his sister, as they rarely saw things the same way. She ridiculed him for being quiet when he ought to be loud.

"I suppose I can join you for a measure."

Edward followed her out to the great balcony creaking in the heavy wind. Shouts echoed through the forest, and cold spears were waved about as the Evergreen Host tried to herd the rippling, snowy creature away from Timber Castle.

"I'm merrily ubbersnugged!" Ever shouted over to him, even though he was not far and there was no need to shout. "Have you ever seen a snowsquatch like that one?"

Edward smiled at her enthusiasm but found the moment of joy drain as he watched the snow creature burst through the trees, knocking over a sturdy oak in the process. A thing like that would plow right through the beams holding up the castle below them. But that was not what captured his worry.

"That's not a snowsquatch." Edward's confusion brimmed the air.

"Of course it is!" Ever was yelling again. "Fall, squatch! Fall!"

"It's..." Edward tilted his head to hear better, certain he was not imagining the bellows that sifted through the trunks like a chilly Winter wind. "It's *talking*."

"What?" Ever made a face; she was partly hanging over the ledge of the rickety wooden rail to watch, and Edward snatched the back of her garland dress to yank her safely beside him where she belonged.

"It's alive, Ever!" he said suddenly. "Pinespittle...That thing is *speaking*."

Before he realized what he was doing, Edward charged down the stairs into the castle lobby where the doors had been propped wide open so the Council of Pines could marvel at the performance of the Evergreen Host. "Stop!" Edward yelled, racing out the doors.

Most of the Host did not hear him, so he called again, "Stop! By command of your prince!" And *that* got their attention.

Ropes were fastened around the white creature's limbs. It thrashed and pulled against the soldiers' hold, spitting snowflakes into the air. A wide path seemed to have been forged through the woods from the snowsquatch's running, and Edward made a face at it, disturbed.

"Tell me, creature. What are you truly? You're certainly not a squatch," he asked it.

The Evergreen Host began exchanging glances, not subtly enough. But Edward ignored them and fought the impulse to tug his emerald cape tighter around his shoulders.

The creature's arms of snow and ice came down to its sides. The thing stared at the Green prince. Edward stared back. "Why were you yelling my name?" Edward then asked.

The snowsquatch had gone quite still; no more fuss. No more anger. No more fight.

"You can hear me, Prince?" it asked. And it was then that Edward realized the rest of the Evergreen Host, the Council of Pines at his back, and every other Green soul in the woods could *not* hear the creature's voice. Edward wanted to ask how it was possible that only he could hear it speak, but he was afraid of the audience now.

"I've come to give you a path," the creature of snow said, raising a glittering hand toward the uprooted trees and branches littering the forest floor behind him.

"Yes…it seems you've made quite a muddle of the forest," Edward remarked, then blushed.

"Shall I take you with me, Prince?"

The creature waited, and it was clear the Evergreen Host were getting impatient, tugging harder on their ropes, inching closer with their spears and axes poised.

"Who sent you?" Edward abandoned all hope for his reputation. But he was certain he had heard this not-snowsquatch shouting his name through the woods.

"If you come with me, I shall take you to the one who sent me."

But Edward's eyes fell to the men at his right and left and back and front. Men who stared at him, waiting for a command. Men who served his father and may soon serve him.

And his sister watching from the balcony where he had left her.

"You shall not have me." Edward spoke in his princely voice now, one of decisions and authority and a pinch too much false confidence. He turned to the Host. "Release him. He will go back to where he came from."

"Release him? But Your Highness, he's an abomination! No snowsquatch should look like this," one of the soldiers objected.

"Do as I say, or I'll turn you to pinespittle."

With one last glance at the creature, Edward turned and

marched his way back into Timber Castle where guests judged him with their eyes and hearts, splitting out of the way to make a river of open floor space for him to pass.

Their future king.

The heir they now thought was mad.

Midday arrived with the clash and clamour of spears, axes, wooden flag poles, and gongs. Torches and barrel fires illuminated the already sunlit, glassy floor of the outdoor arena where the Silver Jubilee Renewal would take place. Edward fiddled with his gloves, eyes cast to the rink that would become a king's deathbed on this day. The fragrances of damp soil and smoke filled his lungs with a dull energy, turning his nerves to fumes.

Ever had not been permitted to come to the Silver Jubilee Renewal. She was too young to watch. Too young to be a queen, too. Not that it would come to that.

This was a day celebrated with feasting, music, and the beating of animal skin drums. A day eagerly anticipated for the past twenty plus five seasons since the last Renewal had taken place. But it was rapidly transforming into the worst moment on Edward's timestring.

His father would win. The King of the Pines *had* to win.

Edward could not be King yet.

In the field beyond the rink, tongues of snow lapped at the air, turning much of the view into a wall of white. There was no seeing past the boundary of the kingdoms where the woods stopped and the rolling slopes of the Red Kingdom began. Many men and women had died at this border, *for* this border, *because of* this border. Many men would expect Edward to avenge those losses by driving younger folk into battle in the seasons to come.

A form stood amidst the flurries in the distant field, and Edward stilled as he realized it was the tall shape of a giant man that looked remarkably like a snowsquatch...but was not one.

Edward glanced to his right and left, but no one else seemed to notice the creature hiding in plain sight, camouflaged against the squalls at his back. The abominable snowsquatch stood without a wave or salute, and it occurred to Edward that the creature was waiting for something.

But what?

Even amidst the ruckus of the crowds and the glory of the Silver Jubilee Renewal, Edward knew there could only be one thing that creature was waiting for; the creature that had spoken to Edward when no one else had heard. Who had called his name in the woods.

Edward scoured the faces in the crowd for Shanely's. After the professor had left Edward to go to bed on the eve past, he had not shown himself at breakfast, Edward realized. And from what he could see, the professor was not sitting among this shouting throng now.

Edward stood as realization dawned on him: the teacher Edward had known for such a measure and learned to love as a non-blood-related uncle, had *left*. Shanely had fled Timber Castle.

But why? Because he had told Edward to run? Edward would not have tattled on the man to the King of the Pines. Did Shanely not trust Edward to keep his mouth shut? Or was it something else?

The Green Prince's gaze fired back to the not-snowsquatch in the field, but the creature had vanished.

Trumpets blasted over the ice, and Edward realized he was the only folk standing. He sank to his throne, a throne that mirrored the set of smaller thrones across the ice where a pair of child-princes sat in warm crimson capes, one with bright ivory hair. Ever had been considered too young to watch this absurd tradition, but it seemed the Crimson King had not thought it unsuitable for his own sputtlepun children who were barely old enough to run or hold a sword.

Since Ever was back at the castle, and Edward's mother had passed ten seasons ago, and his father was preparing to battle the Crimson King, the Green Prince sat alone. Alone, as he had always perhaps been among the Greens.

The kings of the Renewal marched onto the ice, a silver sword in the hand of the King of the Pines and a gold sword in the slender grip of the younger, fitter Crimson King. The Crimson King was perhaps only a few seasons older than Edward himself, with soot-black hair and a cruel look in his purple eyes.

Banging cymbals and shaking bells magnified when the kings raised their swords like metal flags in the air. The Crimson King tipped his blade toward the Ruby Legion, who batted their spears and swords against their copper armour. Likewise, the King of the Pines saluted the Evergreen Host who shouted his praises and struck their own wooden breast-plates.

Edward felt the rush of the wind off the faraway fields bite at his cheeks and slide down his collar. He shifted in his seat. And he realized he could *not* watch this gruesome tradition. He could *not* honour a pointless death or glorify the hatred that saturated the air whenever these two kingdoms met. Ever had been the one deemed too young to attend, but Edward was certain now that he was the one not ready.

He sprang from his throne and barrelled down the stairs of the platform amidst the chaos. He was not sure if any souls noticed, if he was being called after, or if he was being pursued. Edward Green would not be King of these beasts, he would not lead them into battles against the Reds, no matter what it cost him.

All he could think of now was Ever in Timber Castle. He had to make his sister see sense, before it was too late.

Edward's heavy woodsman boots clamoured over the nests of sticks and stones on the forest floor until he reached the poorly guarded front entrance of the castle. He made a disgusted noise at how easy it might have been for the Ruby Legion to sneak across the borders and burn the castle to cinders using the Silver Jubilee Renewal as a distraction.

In the distance, sharp cries, screams, and cheers erupted over the forest, and Edward came to a halt.

The Silver Jubilee Renewal had ended early.

Someone had won.

THIRDLY

Edward felt a pinch of his spirit slip away as he ran into the castle.

"Ever!" he called into the vaulted heights of the lobby. "*Ever!*"

He had assumed she would wait by the entrance to hear the outcome of the Renewal, but she was nowhere in sight. He could not leave her here to face the kingdom alone; Ever Green could not be responsible for slaying the Crimson King if their father had failed to.

Edward banged his way up the stairs until he reached her chambers. He came to a halt when he found her there, sitting at her window, unguarded by even a single Host soldier. How careless it all was. How much trust did the Greens have in the sanctity of the Silver Jubilee Renewal, to not even station guards around the castle in case the Reds cheated on their vows of ceasefire?

"Ever." Edward looked around her room, trying to decide what to collect for their journey.

But when his sister turned, she did not have tears in her eyes, even though she must have heard the cheers from her window. "Did he win?" she asked. "Our father?"

Edward swallowed, hard. "I don't know."

Ever Green's cold, iron eyes narrowed. "You don't know? You...Pinespittle...you *left*?!"

"Ever, run from here with me. I know we are different in a measure of ways, but you're all I care about here. They'll expect us to avenge our father if he's dead. They'll expect us to rage in the wars and be a part of the savagery that's tearing our kingdom's soul apart." Edward stepped in and readied his outstretched hand to receive her. "Come with me, Sister. Let's get away before we're drowned in their war."

Ever stared at him. Tears did rise this time, but Edward had a feeling it was for a different reason than fear of their father's death. "You're a coward," she whispered, and Edward's hand fell back to his side. "What makes you think I would want to leave?" Ever moved toward the sputtlepun-sized wooden suit of armour by her bed—a suit fastened with lace, pearls, and rare stones. "What makes you think I don't *want* to join the war?!"

As she screamed it, Ever drew the silver blade from its sheath and pointed its tip at Edward. "I'll not let you leave, Prince. Traitor. *Coward.*" Her words cut into Edward like the blade itself. "Fight me if you wish to go. But I will not let you walk out of here unscathed."

Fear flitted over Edward's features, but mostly, over his heart. Not for himself.

"Sister. I wish I'd brought you to the villages to meet the folk who changed my heart." Edward drew his own sword. He would not fight this girl who was far too consumed to understand what she was doing, or the ties she was cutting. But as she lunged for him with a feminine battle cry, the Green Prince deflected easily and tripped his sister to put her into a heap on the floor.

"I love you, Ever. Even if you don't see it." They were his parting words as Edward stepped back out the door of her chambers. "I'll come back and prove it to you," he shouted as he left—one of his first shouts in many seasons.

But when he was halfway down the hall, aiming for the back entrance of the castle without a single item of provision or food for his escape, Edward heard his sister's scream in return:

"Don't ever come back here, Edward Green!"

The snowstorm in the field was a monster all on its own. Edward shielded his face as he tried to wade through the lake of flurries where he had last seen the abominable snowsquatch. He had been at it for nearly an hour, calling into the cold air, before a pair of icy hands grappled his mid-section and tore him right up from the ground.

The Prince of the Pines shrieked as he was tossed over a snowy shoulder, his sword slipping from his fingers. He watched the blade get left behind as the not-snowsquatch trampled over the field in a run. All Edward could do was hold on.

When the icy wind finally ceased its ruffling of Edward's hair, he opened his eyes to find himself being carried into a cave. The not-snowsquatch dumped him in a pile by the entrance, and Edward scrambled further in to escape the cold. His hands trembled—he had forgotten gloves. Without a word, the white monster turned and disappeared back into the howling gales, and Edward blinked.

"*Pinespittle*," he cursed, glancing down at his blueing fingers. He had no weapon, and now he was alone in a cave he could not guess the location of.

"I'd ask how your trip was, but I can see you didn't enjoy it much."

Edward spun on his knees at the voice that trickled from the cave's depths where shadow concealed the face of the man speaking. But Edward knew that voice. He had learned most of what he knew from that voice.

"Shanely? Please tell me that's you."

The professor hobbled from the darkness, wrapped in knit blankets unlike the scratchy wool sheets and quilts of Timber Castle. Shanely's maize eyes glowed against the darkness.

"Frosty will bring us wood for a fire. He won't come in here while it's lit though. Poor thing will melt in the heat." Shanely rattled on as though all was normal, the way he had most mornings when he had dragged carts of books and tea into Edward's chambers.

"Shanely, what sort of muddle have you gotten me into?" Edward drove to his feet. "I reckon I wouldn't have run unless you'd suggested it."

"You would have run anyway, son. Quit nattering. You never wanted to be King. You hate the way they feast and toss away the leftovers while the villagers go hungry."

Edward's mouth twitched. He chose not to respond.

Suddenly, a pile of twisted branches tumbled into the

mouth of the cave and Edward leapt away before he was crushed. The not-snowsquatch grunted a laugh from where he stood then turned to disappear into the storm again.

"Ah, firewood. Excellent."

"Professor," Edward tried again. "What am I to do now? I've just left my home. My life."

"A life you didn't want, Edward," Shanely reminded him. "And for the love of Winter, settle down and start this fire before we both freeze to ice." The old man plunked down on a boulder to wait, and Edward set his jaw. But he got to work, using a method that Shanely had taught him a measure ago that was different from how the huntsmen often did it—with stones, not sticks.

In only a pinch, the fire was lit.

Shanely gave a nod of approval, a proud look sneaking across his face. Edward did not feel like a pupil now however, not out here on the cusp of this windy field while his kingdom felt so far away.

"What am I supposed to do, Shanely?" Edward asked again now that warmth was breathing into the corners of the cave. Shanely's face glowed sunrise-yellow, the creases in his skin seeming deeper with the shadows.

"That's up to you, son. What would you have done if Frosty hadn't just found you in the field? Where would you have gone?"

Edward glanced out toward where the not-snowsquatch was lost to the dance of pale flakes in the air. "I suppose I hadn't thought that far."

"Sure, you have. This is not the first time you've thought of running. You must have had some place in mind where you would hide."

"Well…" Edward folded his arms, feeling the bitter touch of shame on his cold skin. "I had a friend in Bellbun I imagined I would stay with. But he's gone now."

"Ah. I see. And where did *he* go when he ran?" Shanely rubbed his hands together, then flattened them toward the heat of the fire.

"I don't know. But I imagine if I'm going to have any chance at helping my sister during my timestring, he would be the one to help me do it. He could sing away the storms. Make people see things another way. And I suppose what I want the most now is for people to see things a different way." Edward's eyes fell to the cave floor. "Charlie was his name."

"Charlie, you say. And you claim he sings away the storms?" Shanely glanced off in thought. "Hmm. How interesting."

Edward's glance darted up. "Do you know of him?" he asked.

"I can't be certain," the professor admitted. "But I know of a nameless pair hiding in plain sight in the Red Kingdom who are muddling quite a few buttons in the Crimson Court. Their identities remain a mystery and no one can ever seem to find where they hide to scribe their hymns and grow their numbers, but…I know an ally or three of theirs. In fact, some might say I *am* one of their allies."

"What do you mean?" Edward inched closer to the fire.

Shanely paused, considering. "I've vowed to keep it a secret, for their sakes. But I think this is a secret you should know, Edward. I think if you want to aid them in their fight to open the eyes of the blind, you should perhaps know where they gather their underground cathedral."

"Their…what?"

Shanely stood from the rock, no longer the joking old man who tested his pupil, but someone who Edward realized had risked his life to save him. "They believe that a young, miracle-working man named Elowin is the King of Truth the ancient Volumes of Wisdom promised would come. I did not tell you many stories of the True King of Winter, but I know I slipped some scrolls into your reading with your morning apple tea."

"Why?" Edward staggered back a step. He had not heard utters of the forgotten sacred truths in many seasons. Not since Shanely had taken him to the Fountain of Wishes.

"Because I believe Elowin is who he says he is. The one the ancient prophets claimed would be sung to sleep by a magic drum on his day of birth and would one day be crowned with a garland wreath of thorns. Those same prophets called him other names in their texts, but he was given the name *Elowin* at birth."

"Pinespittle, Shanely, I thought those were just stories!" Edward did not know what to believe now. Perhaps Shanely was as crazy as the other teachers all nattered.

"The Green Kingdom tried to bury the past to make way for new ideas. Son, I think if you want to know for sure you should find your friend, Charlie."

Edward stared at his professor. "Why do you believe one of that nameless pair in the Red Kingdom is my friend, Charlie? Charlie would never be foolish enough to go there."

"One of the pair is a choir director and a writer of hymns. One whom the believers say *sings away the storms*."

For a measure, Edward did not move. Even when Frosty returned and inched into the cave to inform them the storm was settling, Edward only whispered a "*Thank you*" to the not-snowsquatch.

Shanely's maize eyes lifted. Despite the weight in the cave, the old man grinned. "Ah. Now that is why you belong off the Green throne, Edward," he said, shuffling over the stone floor to see the dwindling storm for himself. "Because you can hear Frosty speak. And only those who have the Truth inside of them can hear the voices of the ancient creatures, of animals, and even nature." But Shanely paused as another thought crossed his mind, and he turned back to Edward, brows tugged inward.

"Do you want to know how the Silver Jubilee Renewal ended, son?" he asked.

The news would reach Edward soon enough, but still...

"No."

FOURTHLY

They were an unusual triad: the once-prince, the rumoured-mad professor, and the abominable snowsquatch. They travelled at night when the stars were the brightest, staying out of sight and carrying the Winter wind in their strides. It took a day or three to venture across the snow meadows and to emerge from the firefly-speckled forests on the brim of the Green Kingdom.

"You'll need a peasant's name," Shanely said as they arrived at the cusp of an unguarded Red Kingdom village, beyond which, there was no going back.

Edward's head spun with the warning the professor had offered on their walk—that if they were caught in the Red Kingdom, Edward's fate would be far worse than the one he had left behind in the woods.

"I already have a peasant's name," the Prince of the Pines replied. He dragged a finger down the strap of his satchel stuffed with supplies Shanely had managed to smuggle out of Timber Castle before the Silver Jubilee Renewal had even begun.

Shanely raised a brow. "Let's have it, then. What is your peasant's name, Prince?"

Prince. King. Green. Edward was none of those things now.

"In the villages they called me Edward Haid," he admitted. "I think I'll stick with that."

"Ah. I see. Good choice," Shanely said as he stepped into the town.

Chandeliers of red ribbons hung proudly above doors, and scarlet murals covered the walls of pale buildings. Smoke and wild berry scents burned on a nearby public stone fireplace where a handful of villagers huddled around to natter and keep warm.

Shanely pulled a scrap of parchment from his coat and squinted at the number etched upon it.

"Oh, for the love of Winter." Edward snatched the parchment to read it himself. "You managed to grab a jar of iceberry pudding, but you couldn't pack your spectacles?"

A low rumble of laughter rolled from the not-snowsquatch. The creature slinked away to hide in the trees and wait.

"It says room four hundred plus six," Edward told the professor as he handed the parchment back.

"Ah, yes. I should have remembered that." Shanely stuffed the slip back into his coat and snorted at the sight of a bow-embellished reindeer emerging from behind a magnificent gold sleigh. "This kingdom is all bells and whistles," he muttered.

"Shall I ask someone how to find this room?" Edward asked, eyeing the villagers.

"No, son. Don't breathe a word of this number. Or that we're looking for a room. If we're meant to find it, we will." Shanely glanced through the houses toward the bush as if trying to spot where Frosty had settled.

"That doesn't make a pinch of sense." Edward rubbed his temples, certain they were doomed. "Do you think we ought to head—"

A loud laugh swallowed Edward's words, and the once-prince and the professor alike lifted their gazes to a muscular, dark-skinned man by the incense fire. The man was taller than anyone Edward had ever met, but the most startling of the man's features was the delicate set of purple wings fluttering at his back. Golden dust floated off him, and a thin band of nobility rested around the man's temple.

"What in all of Winter is that?" Edward whispered.

"Hmm. I feel I should know this. I've read about a good measure of Winter species, but I just can't seem to remember things like I used to—*Edward*?!"

Edward marched to the fire with scent-riddled smoke, tugging the collar of his cloak tighter at his throat to ensure it hid his clothes, even though he had cast off his green back in the cave.

"Hello there. My...*grandfather* and I are looking for an Inn. Do any of you happen to know where we might stay a day or three?" He flashed a lovely smile.

"Kingsblood, did you just come out of the forest?" The closest villager's eyes roamed over Edward's cloak and all the bits of dirt and twigs attached to it.

"Um...no—"

"Wait a measure...you look familiar," a youthful folk said, turning to face Edward fully.

Behind the young fellow, the large, muscled male's eyes flickered, a smile finding his mouth. "Well, he *should* look familiar. He's the Prince of the Pines," he said.

Edward's blood froze in his veins. His mind tumbled through ideas of what might have given him away, and worse, what these villagers might do to him now.

"I am *not*," Edward lied, backing up until he bumped into Shanely. "You're mistaken."

"I was at the Silver Jubilee Renewal, Prince. I saw you," the same villager objected. "You're the enemy prince. The new King of the Pines."

The new King of the Pines...

Edward swallowed. "Shanely," he said in a quiet voice. "Run."

The old man did not waste time arguing. He turned on his heel and sprint-hobbled through the buildings. Edward drew a short sword from beneath his cloak, a threat to any of the villagers who'd try to follow. "You will not speak to anyone of what you've seen," he said, his voice carrying authority.

But it was not enough; the villagers all began to laugh.

"I will bring an army of the Evergreen Host into this village if I hear you've told anyone you've seen me," Edward threatened a time again, and this time it was the large man with wings who chuckled.

The goliath drew around the fire and gazed down at the once-prince, blanketing Edward in his shadow. Edward spun to chase after Shanely, but the man caught his collar and held him tight. "Threats, Prince?" He smiled. "Weren't you ever told to never threaten a fairy?"

Edward's eyes widened, but the man stopped, his bright eyes flickering to something across the street. Edward craned his neck to see.

There stood Shanely, wind rippling back his coat. "Did you really think the Prince of the Pines would have travelled alone?" the professor called.

"Shanely, what are you doing?!" Edward tried to whisper, but the buildings rattled, and the villagers began to shift and gasp. Around the bend came Frosty, and the once-prince blanched.

With the abominable snowsquatch came a raging tongue of ice and snow like a whip, lashing the scented fire to death and making the nearby villagers scream. Frosty *roared*; a reverberating, bone-shuddering sound that echoed into the forest. He kicked at obstacles in his path, pounding through wood and rattling stone.

The fairy dropped Edward's collar and the once-prince hit the ground, watching as the fairy drew a long, dual-bladed sword from where it had been fastened to his back. "By the sharpest wind…" the man muttered.

"Run, Prince!" Frosty growled, his breath dispatching frost onto every surface of the street.

"Don't tell him to *run*—" the fairy objected, but Frosty's whip sliced through wind and air, and the fairy dropped to a knee and pulled around a bronze shield.

Edward scrambled back on his limbs until Shanely's hands came beneath his shoulders and hoisted him to his feet.

"Let's go!" Edward turned the old man for the alley, but Shanely stared back at the fairy and the not-snowsquatch with furrowed brows as they struck and parried.

"He could *hear*," the professor said.

Edward did not wait around to natter. He tugged the old

man back into the trees, back into the woods, back to the wind and animals and wild where they belonged.

They raced for a good measure of time before Shanely was too winded to continue. Edward sat the man on a boulder and leaned against a tree himself to catch his breath. He dabbed a bead of sweat from his brow.

"Will Frosty be able to find us?" His words came out chopped.

"I hardly know," the professor admitted with a hand against his chest. "I hardly know anything now, son."

Edward slid down the trunk to sit, grabbing his hair in a fist. "I cannot hide here, Shanely. They know me. Every-where I go, people will know me," he said, shaking his head in disbelief. "Perhaps if I hadn't attended the Silver Jubilee Renewal the Reds wouldn't have known who I was. But thousands of folk were there, and I sat before them all. The Crimson King will find out soon enough that I'm a peg out of its shell in the Red Kingdom."

Shanely lifted from the rock and came to slump in the snow across from Edward. "We cannot go back to Green," he said. "They'll strip you of your title and punish you. You'll be seen as a coward."

"I *am* a coward!" Edward shot back. "I ran away from the Silver Jubilee Renewal because I could not stand to watch. I ran away from my responsibility to the kingdom because I did not want it. And I ran away from…"

Ever.

"Son," Shanely's hand found his shoulder. "No one should have to suffer through all those things as you were expected to. We will find *Room Four Hundred Plus Six*. We will find your friend Charlie."

Edward looked to his hands, red and bruised from how tight he'd gripped the half-sword. "I was not made for this, Professor. I was not made for war."

"I know."

Birds began singing in the trees and Edward leaned his head against the trunk to watch them. If only those birds knew the troubles that came with being a Rime Folk. If only Edward knew the peace of being a bird.

It was midday before they risked venturing into another village, and this time Edward kept his hood up and Shanely did the talking. They spent until dusk asking the locals about inns, braving whispers about a choir director, trying to find an ally amidst the Red Kingdom hustle. They had visited ten plus two inns before the skies had melted to deep blue, and they were forced to return to the woods to sleep in the cold.

FIFTHLY

The sunrise's kiss of gold hadn't yet spilt over the horizon when Edward was harshly shaken awake. Shanely's maize eyes were wide overtop of him.

"They've come for you, Edward! The Ruby Legion has flooded the woods!" The professor's whisper sailed above the cold. "You must run, son!"

Edward's mind was clouded with sleep when he scrambled to his feet. "We'll run together!" he said, but Shanely shook his head.

"No time for us both. I'll say I was alone."

Edward fell silent, but Shanely mustered a kind smile.

"Perhaps in a season or three, you can become a mentor to someone as I have been to you. And you can give everything you have to another deserving folk."

The once-prince stared at his teacher, his oldest friend, as wisps of crimson capes began to peek from the trees a stone's-toss away. This was the man who had become his true father in their seasons together. Both their eyes glistened until Shanely exhaled and shoved the Prince of the Pines into the evergreens.

"Don't come back this way, Edward."

Edward fumbled the first step or three until he collected his balance. He was not as fast as most—he had learned that while racing the boys of Bellbun—but that did not distract him now.

Green needles slapped his coat and cheeks. Sap caught his sleeves. Pale breaths curled into the air around him as he raced across the Red Kingdom border with no destination. A commotion rustled the woods a measure behind, and he placed a fist over his mouth to conceal his cries as he imagined the old man being found, taken, or worse.

He should have never left the Green Kingdom. He should have tried to stop the war from his father's throne, even if it would have been a dreadful undertaking that might have turned his people against him. Being despised would have been better than having his timestring snuffed out for good.

A rock caught his ankle and Edward fumbled onto a bed of frozen moss, palms scraping the undergrowth. He panted and blinked away salty tears, wishing he could go back and fix it all. Wishing for the Fountain of Wishes. For a miracle.

But what he found instead was a pair of leather boots stepping onto the moss before him, the hem of a bloodred cape scraping the ground.

Edward's gaze climbed the man's frame to a copper helmet and silver spear. "Pine-pup," the Ruby Legionnaire muttered is disgust.

Half a dozen hands seized Edward's coat, dragging him back up to his feet and wrenching back his arms to tie them with wire. The once-prince looked from face to face, tree to tree, bush to bush, but he did not see Shanely's maize eyes among any of it.

The wire cuff chiselled into Edward's wrists as the Ruby Legion led him out of the forest and hoisted him onto a golden sleigh. Villagers watched from beneath gold-dusted eyelids and pomegranate-adorned hats: The Green Prince. Their enemy. The boy meant to be their rival king.

Edward's heart thundered in his chest when the sleigh pulled up to the great white palace of the Reds. He was pulled from the sleigh and ushered through a side entrance where his wire bindings were removed and replaced with heavy iron chains. The chains dragged along the floor as the group made their way through basement passages, up a stair or three, and into a room filled with blinding light the colours of rosy stained glass.

Edward squinted up at the dais upon which four thrones sat, all full—two young boys, a woman who snarled at his pine needle-riddled clothes, and...the Crimson King himself. The man who had just won the Silver Jubilee Renewal.

Edward's shuddering ceased, and he found himself standing taller. "Murderer," he said—a word that seemed to reverberate through the quiet room and stir the nobles crowded at the sides.

The king raised a dark brow. "Am I, Prince?"

Edward tugged at the iron cuffs on his arms.

"What has happened to my professor?" he asked, stealing a look around to see if the old man had turned up here.

He did not find Shanely, but he did spot a girl standing among the nobles with penetrating gray eyes. A ring of keys—all different colours—was attached to her belt. The intensity with which she stared at him made Edward shift his footing.

"I know nothing of a professor." The king's raspy voice pulled Edward's gaze back.

"He speaks of the aged folk we found in the woods," a Ruby Legionnaire offered. "The man has been turned back into snow."

The news slammed into Edward's gut like a lumber wheel. The once-prince's speck of bravery dissolved into the red carpet below his boots, and he released an unprincely sound. "He's dead?" Edward whispered.

"Kingsblood, I'm certain the aged spinbug *wanted* us to snuff out his timestring," the Legionnaire snorted. "He merrily laughed at us until his last breath."

Edward's heart leaked its last drop of hope.

"How riddlesome," the Crimson King said, rising from his throne. "Now, I think we ought to gift the Prince of the Pines our finest cage."

Chuckles and murmurs flitted across the crowd of nobles. Edward glanced at them in time to realize that the girl with the gray eyes was the only Red not laughing.

Moments later, Edward found himself in the lobby of the Red Kingdom palace, being shoved into a cage of steel and copper bars. Scarlet liquid pooled at his boots, splashing as he stumbled in, and he faltered.

"What is…" He hardly wanted to guess what the pool was made of.

"Happy Red Holiday," a Legionnaire snorted in laughter

as he slammed the cage door shut. "Enjoy you gift!"

Edward was left in the quiet room where he noted ten plus four other cages of the same sort as his—only the other cages were all along the walls. His was in the centre of the lobby; a grand spectacle. Burly men shifted behind their bars, their wooden armour grinding as they tried to adjust in their boxes.

"Pinespittle…" the once-prince whispered. For, surrounding him in these dreadful cages were men in pine garlands, leathers the colours of the forest, thick boots meant for muddy terrain, and wood-toggled coats. These men were Green. These men were *his* people.

And with the way they all stared, Edward did not doubt they recognized who he was. By now, they must have known how the Silver Jubilee Renewal had ended, since the Crimson King was still alive.

Shame prickled Edward's cheeks as he cast his glance to the inky pool of red paint at his ankles. Perhaps the Green prisoners expected him to save them. Perhaps they wondered if the Evergreen Host would charge the Red Kingdom palace to save their Green *king*, and they might all be rescued in the process.

How disappointed they would all be when the Evergreen Host never came.

SIXTHLY

A day or three had passed before Edward was pulled back out of the cage. In that time, he had avoided speaking to the Green prisoners as much as he could. At any noise, the Ruby Legionnaires threatened to poke them with their spears—to Edward's shame and relief—and so he did not tell his Green woodsmen why he was captured or give false promises of their freedom to come.

The once-prince was led out into the bright sunlight where hundreds of horses and reindeer awaited, some strapped to sleighs, others with crimson-caped riders. From the back of the Crimson King's buck, a rope was fastened to the muzzle of another deer—this was where Edward was led.

The guards at Edward's elbows halted him before the creature and Edward swallowed a grunt as he realized what the Crimson King planned to do. The Prince of the Pines would be forced to ride into battle at the Crimson King's back like a chained snowpup. To make a show of the Green

Prince as his prisoner.

Snickers erupted across the army of Ruby Legion soldiers—men and elves—as they noted Edward's reaction.

A tug of his chains forced his wrists to lift, and a girl swept in before him with piercing gray eyes, light hair, fair and lovely. And very, *very* Red in her choice of clothing.

Edward eyed the hem of her cherry dress sweeping the snow while she drew a key from her pocket. Her brows were furrowed as though she were upset. Combined with the sharpness of her eyes, it was just as unnerving as it had been in the throne room when he had first noticed her watching him.

"You have quite a deadly stare," Edward remarked as the lock clicked and the first iron cuff slid off his wrist.

"I suppose I do not like fibbers," she whispered, snatching his second cuff to draw it closer. Her key slid into the lock, and she twisted it. She scowled at a Ruby Legionnaire who stepped in to assist when the key resisted, daring him to suggest she needed help doing her job.

But Edward made a face. "I have not fibbed."

"Not to *me*, Prince," she said, wrenching on the key. Finally, the second lock snapped, and the cuff loosened. But her sharp eyes lifted. "Or shall I call you Edward *Haid*?"

Edward faltered. "Where did you hear that name?!"

Falling snow found a resting place on the girl's hair as she blinked. "I cannot save you, Prince. Even if Charlie Little wishes I would. You are on your own—I will not risk exposing my cathedral," she said. "May the forces of Winter find a way to save you before you meet this fate." She nodded to the Ruby Legion army at her back.

Edward's eyes were wide as the girl whisked away, disappearing into the Red crowds who stood by to see the Ruby Legion off. He scanned the people, the elves, the slender ones with bright-white skin, half-sized creatures, and all the rest, looking for a familiar face. But if Charlie Little was in fact in the Red Kingdom, he was not in this crowd.

A fibber. Yes, Edward realized he was a fibber, indeed. He had never told Charlie who he was. It seemed Charlie had figured out a thing or three now though.

"Do you know how to ride, Pine-pup?" The Crimson King's windy voice drew Edward back to the Ruby Legion shuffling impatiently, itching to leave.

"Of course," Edward muttered. Such a question was an insult to a born and raised prince.

Legionnaires hovered close as he climbed onto the reindeer's back, and once again his hands were tied with a wire. The Red King sneered from atop his mighty beast, one with glorious antlers that pierced the skies like claws of bone. A copper helmet was placed over the man's black hair.

"To the frontlines!" the king called over his army, who called back with an earth-rattling cry that heated Edward's blood.

As the Legionnaires took off, deer fleeing after deer and horses snarling mist into the air, Edward gripped the reins of his creature and felt his heart shred to ribbons.

Edward Green was going to the one place in all of Winter he had tried so desperately to run from.

The sky had morphed to a blazing silver, the sun desperate to break through the clouds, glowing behind the haze like white embers. Edward kept his eyes on that horizon, unable to look right or left where men and elves hoisted blades, bows, and spears.

Over and over, he prayed and wished that Ever would not be at the frontlines like she had claimed she wanted to be, that she would not see him this way, and that she would not be crushed by the sight of another great victory for the Crimson King.

Edward's gaze finally settled on the army around him. And without another thought about it, he flung himself off his deer.

His shoulder struck the trodden snow, twisting out of shape. He released a cry as he rolled to avoid being trampled by the next reindeer and then the next. He scrambled to his feet during a break in the lines, and a spear pierced weightily into the snow beside him.

Edward spun and raced for the city, past which were the woods, the forests, the trees he belonged in. Sleighs veered off course to avoid running him over, and citizens shrieked as he knocked aside a cart or three, but he did not stop until he slid into an icy alley where he stooped to a knee to catch his breath.

The street behind him erupted with shouts and screams—it seemed the Ruby Legion were racing their sharp-antlered reindeer through the crowds with little mercy for those in their way.

Edward pushed himself up and tore through the length of the alley, panting until he burst through a line of red pine trees and met the quiet woods. Swords sliced through the wild brush behind him, snarls of war-bred deer echoing around the trunks. The once-prince lunged over a brook. He hit a patch of ice on the other side and slid into a fallen log where he toppled over into a heap, chest writhing for air.

Pain heated his kneecaps, but he did not cry or scream. Edward closed his eyes and laid his cheek against the snow to cool it, for, he was relieved he would meet his end this way. The same way Shanely had—in the woods without an audience. A cheerier end than meeting the Crimson King's blade before the watching eyes of his kingdom.

The stomping of the reindeer slowed as the Ruby Legion waded across the brook. Edward thought of the Fountain of Wishes where he had donated the ring his mother had gifted him before she passed. The one she had imparted with an ancient blessing, claiming it would watch over him should he ever find himself in trouble. It was the same day she had appointed Shanely as Edward's professor. Edward had thought a great sacrifice was needed at the well for a great wish, but perhaps he never should have taken the ring off.

The sliding of metal armour filled his ears and Edward braced for the hit in his back, but the sounds of approaching Legionnaires went quiet. Edward's eyes opened.

A great thud shuddered the snow around him. He lifted his head to find two bronze sabatons digging into the earth where a large, muscled man straightened to his full height, and light, violet wings fluttered at his back. The fairy reached over his shoulder and pulled his dual-bladed sword from his back, twisting it once to test its weight as he stepped *over* the once-prince in the snow and took off, splashing through the brook.

Edward rolled to his back to witness the Ruby Legionnaires draw their own weapons, some skidding to a halt, others scrambling back the way they had come. Only one was brave enough to face the winged-man, and that Legionnaire's spear was knocked aside where it toppled into the water.

The wind changed directions, and a howling bellow erupted over the clearing. The melody of snapping branches followed as a great white not-snowsquatch plunged through the evergreens, snow spiralling like antlers at its back.

Edward scrambled to his feet, tripping over rocks and forest brush as he reached his bound arms toward Frosty. The not-snowsquatch's footsteps thundered through the woods as he met Edward, scooping up the once-prince and tossing him over a shoulder to run.

Ice and trunks sped by as Edward was carried off, the cries of the Ruby Legion fading into the forest where they were left to the fairy.

Frosty did not stop until they were swallowed into an ice cave, and there, he dropped Edward to his feet. Teary eyed, Edward looked up at the not-snowsquatch in question, wondering how in Winter he had been found. He opened his mouth to ask, but what came out instead was, "Shanely's gone."

Frosty's body of snow rippled in the wind, but he did not flinch at the news. "Yes. He has graduated to the White Kingdom where he is merry," he said.

"You already knew?" Edward took a step toward the cave entrance but halted as a set of familiar bronze sabatons slammed into the snow before them, blocking off the tunnel's mouth.

The fairy let himself into the cave until he stood before Edward. This close, Edward noticed purple markings on the man's skin that moved with his motions like rippling water. "You," the once-prince said, remembering how the fairy had taunted him in the village.

"Perhaps I got carried away at the fire, Prince. Most fairies cannot help it, you know. You should never threaten a fairy," the man said, folding his burly arms. "I was waiting for you in that village. Right where the Truth whispered you would show up."

"You were waiting for me?" Edward's wrists throbbed where the wires dug in. He squirmed until the fairy's gaze dropped to them. With a swift slice of a dual-bladed sword, the wires snapped loose from Edward's sore flesh.

"Because you are my assignment. Isn't that obvious?" the fairy said. And then to himself, he muttered, "Why does Elowin always give me the *crazy* sputtlepuns?"

Edward glanced to Frosty, but the not-snowsquatch did not object.

"I'm your...*assignment*?" the prince asked.

The fairy sighed. "Well, you prayed didn't you, Prince? At the well? So, here I am." He splayed his arms wide, seeming irritated that Edward still did not understand. "I'm your guardian. You are my assignment," he said again, then he looked back to Frosty when Edward did not reply. "Is he deaf?"

Edward grunted. "I'm not *deaf*." He rubbed the tender

skin at his wrists.

"He too was sent to your aid in the Green Kingdom, which is why things got tangled when we quarrelled in the village over you," the fairy went on, pointing a thumb back at Frosty, "but here we are now, on the same side after all. Your snowy friend could have spared me that icy scotcher-whipping though," he added and shot Frosty a look.

The not-snowsquatch emitted a rumbling laugh.

Edward blinked at the two. A warm hand found his shoulder.

"Edward."

The familiar voice made him whirl.

"Or should I say, *Prince* Edward, you cunning ash-worm?"

Edward's mouth parted, for there stood Charlie Little with the sort of infectious smile that had drawn Edward out of his darkest days a time or three.

"Call me whatever you like, you tree-hugging Pine-pup!" Edward grinned, hardly allowing himself to believe it was true—that he had found Charlie. Or, that Charlie had found him, it seemed.

"Don't give me that sort of power, or I'll name you something dreadful. Like Tootshoot Grumble-Sputt." Charlie dragged Edward into an embrace, soothing the ice in Edward's body and the fear that had spooled his heart rigid.

"I never told you the truth," Edward said. "I should have told you who I—"

"Quiet, Tootshoot. You saved my life once, and now I've saved yours. I imagine we're even," Charlie said. "Besides, living in this cave alone to scribble my psalms is astoundingly boring. I think hiding here might be a measure less insufferable with a friend."

"How did you save my life, Charlie? How did you even know where I was?"

Charlie pulled a pen from his pocket with ink-stained fingers. With it, he pointed at the fairy. "Gathadriel told us. Elowin caught your prayer, and he sent Gathadriel to you, and he told me to wait for you here." His smile returned. "Okay, perhaps I didn't save you *myself*. But I did as I was told, and it turned out right."

A piece of ivory parchment came out of another of Charlie's pockets, and he held the page against Edward's shoulder to scribble a note. "Gathadriel," he said as he wrote. "Will you deliver this to Cora? We must meet again in Room Four Hundred Plus Six—"

"I'm not *your* messenger," the fairy objected.

Charlie sighed. "Fairies." He shook his head.

"My professor had heard of you, Charlie. What is it that you've been doing here?" Edward changed the subject, and Charlie smiled. But his smile fell a pinch.

"We're doing Elowin's work. And it's been a good measure more successful than we imagined, but it is not all good tidings of great joy at present," Charlie admitted. "The Crimson King has offered a large reward for you, Edward. You're a marked folk, and he's just dispatched two of the Ruby Legion's most ruthless hunters after you. Deadly twins with an ear for the forest and an eye for their prey. I fear there's no adequate place to hide from folk like them."

Edward swallowed, imagining that. "I cannot go back to Green," he said.

Charlie's hand returned to Edward's shoulder. "No. You

cannot," he agreed. "You're with us now, Edward. We will use our network of doors to hide you. And if, and when, the Migraithe brothers find us, we will face them together."

LASTLY, AND SO FORTH

The Green once-prince grew in age and spirit over the seasons, aiding Cora Thimble and Charlie Little in their fight against the rising darkness. The Prince of the Pines became one of a dozen great names of the cathedral. One of the dozen voices that altered the course of history and paved the snow for an assembly to rise from the pale Winter cinders. One of the dozen which a terrible Beast of the Winter midnight stars would come to mark and hunt to the ends of the globe without growing tired.

But a greater purpose was within the once-prince's blood. That same purpose which dwells in many of us who choose to believe.

INK

WH**I**PPER

Novella, The Third

Once upon a Winter's snow
A crushed Rime soul began to grow
With a hard spirit and a heart of anger
He cast his hate at every stranger

Gifted, he was, in scribing tales of the stars
But he used his gift to bring upon scars
He served the darkness because he was blind
But soon he would see all he'd left behind

FIRSTLY

The ice-meadow burned crimson where Mikal Migraithe stood with beads of sweat rolling from his brow. The gray skyline jutted up from behind the mountainous cities of the Red Kingdom at his back, streaking the skies with ribbons of pale light from the sun trying to show itself.

Mikal studied the sign in the heavens. The golden burst of light that finally cracked the horizon matched the shade in his eyes—like two hues destined to find each other. There was a story in that sky, trying to tell itself. The young Legionnaire wondered what it might wish to say if given a voice.

"Why is he always so quiet?" Corpian muttered as he sheathed his blade, bringing Mikal's attention back. Corpian was asking Redson, not Mikal.

"He likes to think. Feel free to try it yourself sometime," Redson said to the other Legionnaire as he adjusted his spear.

Corpian glared at the Migraithe brothers but did not poke further, for the Migraithes could be a pair of venomous ashworms when they wished. Twins that could not be told apart, except by how they conducted themselves; Redson, the one who never shut his mouth, and Mikal, the one who rarely spoke at all.

Corpian stalked off toward the Slumber Forest, and Mikal cast his brother a glance of reproach.

Redson grinned.

Four of the most elite Legionnaires had been commission to hunt the Green prince. The Crimson King had pitted Mikal and Redson against Corpian and Sefara, promising a reward of many good tidings to whichever pair could drag the Prince of the Pines to the king's feet. And it seemed the prince had scuttled off to the only place where he knew how to survive: the forest.

Seven weeks plus one half they had been at this; tracking Edward Green through the snow, through the cities, through the glassy mountains. Mikal was ready to end the chase and get back to his writing, his tea, and his warm fires.

"Corpian doesn't seem a pinch worried about the forest," Redson observed as he trudged after the pair in the lead. "Do you think he realizes which forest this is?"

"I imagine he doesn't," Mikal returned, eyeing the fiery-haired Legionnaire approaching the treeline.

"Do you think this forest will tell you one of its *stories*?" Redson asked, pinching a smile.

"Every part of nature tells a story. You just need to *stop talking* long enough to hear it," Mikal said. Redson made a face.

By the time the twins reached the forest's edge, Corpian

and Sefara had disappeared into the trees' shadows. The forest roof was a thick tangle of branches, not allowing snow to get through, leaving the floor bare with cold mud, rocks, and fallen logs with icy moss.

"Careful," Redson whispered as they crept in, each drawing their sword with slow and quiet movements.

They waited. But the forest did not threaten them, try to eat them, or flood their minds with worries as rumour claimed it had done to folk in seasons past. The wisps did not whisper in their ears, nor did the monsters of the woods crawl from their hiding places.

"Hmm." Redson stood to his full height. "I expected something to at least *try* to kill us."

Mikal exhaled a deep breath and opened his ears to hear the hum of the forest's timestring. The forest seemed to grumble something, as though being woken from a peaceful slumber. The sound was too low for Mikal to decipher.

Wind growled over the trees with the gusto of a thousand furious thoughts, deafening Mikal's ear to the tune of the boot-patters racing through the woods up ahead. "He's here. Close by," he whispered to Redson.

Redson peered into the trees. "How does this prince keep getting away from us? I swear he vanished in the city ten plus two days ago when I had him cornered."

"Someone is singing on his behalf," Mikal said. He listened, trying to spot that same musical tenor that had confused them back in the city a time or three already. But he did not hear the songs now. Perhaps the prince had lost his musical friend.

"Singing?" Redson grunted a laugh. "Well then. Troll the ancient Red-yule carol!" he joked.

But the music was not a laughing matter, and Mikal knew as much.

Music told stories, too.

Suddenly, the Slumber Forest hushed. It was as though it had taken in a deep breath and held it. The Migraithe brothers exchanged a look, lifting their weapons.

A twig snapped not far away.

"There!" Redson shouted, pointing far into the woods.

A flash of a cloak swept around a trunk, and Mikal took off after it.

"The sputtlepun is faster than a snowsquatch on syrup!" Redson muttered as he leapt onto a rotted log and raced up its length. He sprang off the end, nearly catching a ribbon of fabric as the figure swept away.

"Left!" Redson shouted back to Mikal, who tore in a new direction to cut the folk off.

Mikal sprang around a thick trunk, grabbing the folk's collar. He caged him tightly against the tree with his forearm. Beneath his elbow, he felt the folk's heart pound at a vicious speed.

"Take down your hood," Mikal commanded, swishing the tip of his blade toward the figure's throat. "You smell of pine trees and woodlands, Prince."

But a low, musical laugh escaped the hood. And when the figure reached to pull it off, Mikal's face fell. For this was not Edward Green but a sputtlepun with simple features; bark-brown hair, a ridiculous smile, and a look in his eye that promised a scheme or three.

"Who are you?" Mikal demanded as Redson came around, huffing to catch his breath.

"I'm a villager who likes to take walks in the woods. Is

that a crime, Legionnaire?" the sputtlepun asked.

"Ragnashuck, why are you *laughing*?" Redson lifted his blade also.

"I laugh at unfortunate times, particularly when I'm nervous. It gets me into a muddle now and again," the folk admitted.

"Why did you run from us?" Redson asked.

"Why did you start chasing me?"

At that, the Migraithe brothers exchanged a glance.

"Do not utter falsehoods. Why are you in these woods really?" Redson got right to it. "Don't you know the dangers of the Slumber Forest?"

"Yes, of course. But forests make the most marvellous music. They're always singing, always telling us a thing with their praise. Quiet, now…" the folk brought a finger up to his lips and closed his eyes. "Can you hear it?" he whispered.

Redson sighed and slid his sword away with a look to say the folk was crazy. But Mikal tilted his head. Hearing the forest's music was not that different than Mikal being aware of the forest's story.

A slow, easy hum slid from the fellow's throat. And deep within that note, Mikal heard a multitude of things: the whistles of wind, the clapping of the leaves, the deep groaning of twisting tree trunks…and something else, too.

A voice.

"Season's greetings, Ink Whipper," it said.

Mikal faltered, the tip of his blade drooping. For all his quiet listening, he had never once heard nature speak like *that*. The song warmed his flesh and awoke his heart. "It's you," Mikal realized. "You're the one with the music."

"Charlie Little." The sputtlepun lifted a hand to introduce himself, but Redson slapped his hand back down.

"I've heard your songs on the wind," Redson cut in. "You nearly deafened me with one in the Scarlet City! Do you know how angry I was, sputtlepun? If you interfere one time more in our hunt for the Green prince, you will be delivered to our king alongside him!"

An untimely smile spread over Charlie Little's mouth, and Mikal's grip tightened on his sword. It was infuriating, even if the fellow could not help himself.

"I think the forest might have other plans," Charlie said.

A thing tapped Mikal's shoulder, and he whirled to find a second figure holding a stick. The figure pulled his hood down. The Migrathe brothers blinked at the set of gold eyes, dark hair, and thick wooden nutshell rings adorning eight fingers plus two thumbs.

Edward Green looked precisely the same as he had at the Silver Jubilee Renewal nearly a quarter ago. The only thing missing was the scowl he'd carried that day.

Redson sprang for the Green prince just as Charlie Little's cloak slid from Mikal's grip. The musical fellow darted into the shadowed woods.

A whirlwind of leaves lifted from the forest floor. The wind pressed against Mikal's temples, dragging its cold fingers across the back of his neck, and he inhaled an ice-cold breath that chilled his throat from the inside.

When he managed to open his eyes against the weather's current, he saw the Green prince step backward into a sinking hole of mud. It sucked him down in a heartbeat.

"Redson!" Mikal called as his brother plunged in after the prince.

The whirlwind ceased, and Mikal Migraithe was left panting in silence. His eyes were round and stung with grains of forest debris.

"Where is my brother?" he whispered to the forest, hoping it might speak to him as it had only a moment ago.

But the forest revealed nothing.

Mikal swallowed and sheathed his sword. Neither the prince nor his brother had come up from the sinkhole. As Mikal waited, a glimmer appeared from the mud. It was like a misty, beckoning hand—nothing like Mikal had ever seen before. He was overcome with the tremendous pull to jump into the sinkhole, as his brother had.

Mikal looked over his shoulder, but the musical fellow was long gone. And so, Mikal inhaled his courage, and he plunged into the mud.

SECONDLY

Everything became black as soot for a moment or three. And then, Mikal found air.

He gasped as his body was propelled through the sludge, and he shrieked when he was spat up from the pool onto a rocky surface.

"Ragnashuck!" he cursed, coughing out a mouthful of dirt.

"Ragnashuck is right!" Redson complained, and Mikal's gaze fired over to his brother standing at the pool's edge, sword lifted and holding a hostage at its point. "He almost got away, brother. He would have escaped us a time again had I not followed him."

A mud-covered Prince of the Pines stole a glance at Mikal panting on the rock.

The branches above spiralled this way and that, speckled with orange leaves. Mikal did not recall seeing such a colour on their way in, and as he dragged himself to his feet, he realized it was because he was not where he had been a moment ago. The pool had spit him out somewhere else entirely.

"Are we still in the Slumber Forest?" he asked the prince.

Edward Green did not speak. A speck of fear crossed his eyes—as it should. He had not come this close to being captured in nearly eight weeks, thanks to his musical friend. A friend, it seemed, who was no longer nearby.

Redson scanned the tree heights, the glimmers of sky that could scarcely be seen through the curled branches, the long rows of trees every which way. "It'll be dusk before we find our way out of here."

They trekked over twig and stone, bush and branch. They trudged until the forest grew so dark, they could hardly see. And after a measure, the trio covered in mud, sticky and heavy, became all around grumpy. Mikal used his sword to feel the darkness ahead as they stepped into it. But eventually, when whispers in the forest told stories of hungry beasts and cave birds, Redson said, "Let's tie up the prince and build a fire."

So, the brothers set the prince alongside a tree and began dragging brush through the dark. Mikal clashed sticks together to find a spark, but the forest was damp, and the air was cold.

After hours of silence, the Green prince finally spoke.

"You won't make a fire that way," he said.

Mikal dropped the sticks to his lap and bristled. It had been a good measure since he had last eaten. Or slept. Or felt warmth.

"Use rocks," the prince said. "Wood is no good in this weather."

Ignoring the enemy prince, Mikal went back to his stick-smashing. Redson too tried to create a spark with twigs, his way. Between the two of them, the Migraithes must have made a hundred fires.

Though, never with damp sticks.

Finally, Mikal tossed the branches to the ground.

"Told you," the prince muttered as he examined the ten plus three rings stacked over his fingers. He appeared bored, sleepy even.

Mikal glared. "How would you light it with rocks, Prince? Enchant them with magic?"

The Green prince burst out laughing. It made Mikal's skin tighten a measure more. "The same way you tried to light a spark with your sticks. Smack them together. Simple."

Mikal was too busy casting the prince a daggered stare, so Redson took it upon himself to try.

When a spark rolled off the rock and landed in the brush, Mikal's glare broke, his eyes dropping to that glow of light altering the atmosphere. The flicker almost went out when it hit the damp sticks, but the leaves caught, and a moment later, a modest fire was born.

Mikal blinked at it. He bit his lips so he would not utter an unmerry thing.

"How did you hide from us this quarter, Prince?" Redson asked, seeming unbothered by the Green prince's arrogant instructions. "Was it your singing friend who confused us?"

The prince found a weak smile. "Charlie sings to the True King of Winter, the one whisperers call *Elowin*. When he sings, mountains move out of the way. That is all." He glanced up at the Migraithe brothers, gold eyes glimmering in the new firelight. "Charlie did not make me disappear."

"Then *how*?" Redson pushed. "Tell us before we deliver you to the Crimson King, and perhaps I won't make you suffer along the walk."

When the Green prince spoke, it was quiet. "There are secret passages in Winter that even you do not know about, Legionnaires."

Redson snorted and slumped back against a rock. "Lies," he decided.

The prince did not reply this time. So, Redson gave his attention to Mikal.

"Brother, tell us a story to pass the time," he said.

Mikal eyed the prince for a measure. But reluctantly, he leaned back too and prepared his voice for that of deep, Winter stories.

"Once upon a Winter's snow…"

Once upon a Winter's snow
There lived a forest, whose roots did grow
Deep within its belly, lay a maze of wood
Only to be escaped if one's intentions were good

"When did those verses come to you, brother?" Redson asked.

Mikal shrugged and plucked a leaf from a twig. "On the hunt," was all he said. But he lifted his gaze to see what the prince thought of the tale and found the Green prince looking rather perplexed.

"You sound like my singing friend, Charlie," the prince said. "You sound like someone gifted."

Crackling lifted from the fire. Mikal cast his brother a look, but Redson simply shrugged.

"But you've chosen to offer your gifts to the darkness. Your spirit is hard, and your heart is full of anger, Legionnaire. I don't excel in intuition, but I know it's easier to hate than to trust. You could scribe tales of the stars, but instead you use your gift to inflict scars upon the Rime Folk. Someday, I hope you see what you're doing."

Mikal felt the coolness and colours drain from his face.

He had written a story yesternight by a late eve's candle. One about a folk who used his gifts for the plans of darkness, with a hard spirit, and who was full of anger. Who, instead of scribing tales of the stars, inflicted scars upon the Rime Folk.

Mikal had written it on a scrap of parchment. He had tucked it away in his pocket for safe keeping.

But he had no idea whatsoever that he had been writing a story about himself.

Once upon a Winter's snow
A crushed Rime soul began to grow
With a hard spirit, and a heart of anger
He cast his hate at every stranger

Gifted, he was, in scribing tales of the stars
But he used his gift to bring upon scars
He served the darkness because he was blind
But soon he would see all he'd left behind

By Mikal Migraithe

It was the middle of the night when the forest spoke to Mikal again. Mikal had not yet slept. Neither had the Green prince, who stared off into the dark corners.

Redson snored like a white frostbull.

Mikal set his writing aside, rolling the scrap of parchment around the ink pen he kept in his pocket. He could not come up with any new verses. It was as though all the stories had gone silent.

"Let me tell you my *story,"* the forest said, and Mikal sat up straighter, fingers curling around his blade's hilt. At first, the Green prince across the clearing did not move, and Mikal thought the prince had not heard the forest speak. That

was, until the prince's gold eyes flickered, and Mikal realized the prince was only pretending.

"Are you making this forest speak to me?" Mikal asked Edward Green.

The prince's face tugged into a sad smile. "I wish I was gifted as *you* are. But I am not. I am not anything important, apart from my family's blood."

Mikal's brows tipped inward, but the forest spoke again. *"I once was lost, but now I'm found. I was blind, but now I see again,"* the forest said, in a tone that mirrored cracking branches and rushing wind.

"Is this a play on words because you've trapped us in your maze of trees?" Mikal guessed, not caring if the prince found it odd that he was conversing with the woods.

"I do not play with words."

"Well, how have you come to speak at all? How did you get breath in your lungs? How are you living?" Mikal said back.

A gentle breeze flittered through the leaves above. It was warm, even though the Winter night was cold.

"Grace. It saved a wretch like me. Perhaps it can save a wretch like you," the forest replied.

Mikal looked back at the prince, but the Prince of the Pines kept his face expressionless. "Only those who have the Truth inside of them can hear the ancient voices of the animals and nature," he said, swallowing. "My old professor said that."

Mikal cringed at the memory of his once-father reciting those "Truths" to him and Redson from sunrise to sunset when they were sputtlepun children. Their father had uttered those religious texts and claimed to be a faithful man of the sacred truths, right up until the day he sold his own two sons to the Ruby Legion for a pocket full of rings.

The Migraithe brothers had not seen their father since. He had never come to buy them back. He had never sent word, or a letter, or a sign that he wished for their return.

"I am not a believer in those ancient scriptures and tales," he assured.

The smile returned to the prince's face. "I was the same. I once believed as you do now."

Mikal was grateful for Redson's loud snort as he rolled over, simply because it broke the tense silence that hung in the air.

"Go to sleep, Prince. We'll be doing a lot of walking at sunrise," Mikal advised, dragging his sword over his lap to rest.

A breath of wind sifted through the trunks, and after another measure of staring, the Green prince did, in fact, drift off to sleep. Mikal kept his eyes on the forest, ready for that cheerful singer to come back and try to rescue his prince-friend.

"And what is your *story, Mikal Migraithe?"* The forest filled his ears, and Mikal released a frustrated sigh. *"You have a story to write. Deep within you. I can hear it."*

"I don't know what you speak of," Mikal hissed.

"Oh, but you do. And you've kept it hidden deep inside you, wrapped in anger. You've ignored it, trying to write other meaningless stories to distract yourself. But the story in you must be told." The forest's whispers reached right into Mikal's mind. He shifted in his seat. *"So, tell it, Ink Whipper. Go tell it on the mountains, over the hills, and everywhere. You will not find freedom until you do."*

"Silence, forest. I'm tired of your nattering." Mikal pulled his hand into a fist and rested his mouth against it, feeling the first weight of the night dim his weary mind.

As it was instructed, the forest went quiet.

It took them the full morning to find their way out of the Slumber Forest. Mikal craved hot tea and spiced meat when they reached the glistening fields of snow. There was no sign of Corpian or Sefara, and Mikal spared them a glance backward, wondering if the forest had done its worst to the other Legionnaires.

There had been no sign of the musical Charlie Little, either.

"Ragnashuck." Redson finally broke the quiet. He rubbed his eyes. "I could go for a cider. And a hot bath."

"Rag-nish-uck? What does that mean?" The Green prince surprised them with the question. He had not made a peep since sunrise. Instead, he had been lost to his thoughts, wringing his wood-wrapped fingers.

"It's an apple-picking term. My brother and I worked in an ice orchard until we were ten seasons old, collecting white apples. It means 'rotten apple' more or less," Redson said.

"We made it up, Redson. It wasn't a real orchard word. We just said it to make the other pickers think we knew more than them," Mikal mumbled.

"Did we?" Redson squinted as he tried to remember.

A silver tongue of snow brushed along the back of Mikal's hand, and he and Redson came to a halt. The Green prince was as still as stone, but a slow smile spread over his face.

Mikal drew his sword.

"Watch your scotcher, brother. We're not alone out here." Redson said what Mikal was thinking.

A short laugh escaped the Green prince. "No. Not at all."

But a voice tore over the field, and the prince's merry face fell as two red-caped Legionnaires came racing over a hill. "Runnn!" one of them yelled.

Mikal grabbed the prince's cloak, forcing him to move.

A creature rose from behind the hill; a snowsquatch beast from nightmarish myth-books.

Corpian fell mid-sprint, but rolled over swinging his blade as the creature of snow stomped over the field. The Legionnaire drove his blade into the snowsquatch's ankle, and the monster released a bone-shuddering growl into the air.

The Migraithes made for the next hill, each with a hand pushing the Green prince forward. Something fired across the sky like a sunbeam, thin violet wings flapping so fast they were nearly invisible.

"It's a frostbitten fairy!" Redson ground out. "Ragnashuck, Prince, what sort of creatures do you keep company with?!"

Mikal calculated the distance to the nearest village. The odds appeared to be against them, but the Migraithe brothers were not considered the most elite hunters for no reason.

"Give me his cloak. And take the prince to that wagon," Mikal instructed, nodding toward an enclosed silver-painted carriage hidden by a reindeer barn. "It's late morning, so the Ruby Legion should arrive here in a minute or three. We need to distract the fairy until then. The Legion will be able to take down the snowsquatch."

The Green prince's face fell. He looked as though he might object, but shouts erupted from Corpian and Sefara battling the snowsquatch.

Redson obeyed, stealing Edward Green's cloak and shoving it into Mikal's hands. Mikal fastened it over his own shoulders and began racing the opposite way, yanking the hood up as he did.

Once upon a Winter's first light
A Legionnaire tricked a fairy in flight
He played a traitor prince so well
What was truth, the fairy could not tell

Once in the village, Mikal took every turn he came to, weaving the fairy's attention through the streets until he lost him. Villagers had gathered to warm their hands and exchange the latest gossip from this morning's Pebble Paper. Mikal swished by them and discarded his cloak upon a barrel of flames. He slipped through the Red-dressed crowds, back to the village's edge where the wagon was still safely tucked away behind the barn.

He knocked lightly on the wagon's door, and it swung open to reveal a gleaming Redson and a pain-faced Green prince.

"Did the Legion kill Frosty?" the prince asked. "Is the not-snowsquatch dead?"

Mikal shrugged. "I imagine so." He backed out of the wagon and snuck into the barn to steal a deer. Once the creature was tied to the wagon's front, he climbed aboard the driver's seat and slapped the bell-studded reins.

To the Red Palace they would go.

THIRDLY

What a presumptuous forest the Slumber Forest was. Mikal could not shake the forest's opinions from his mind. It was as though the forest had reached in and touched something Mikal had missed all his life, something he had been close to finding but had never truly caught. Something he always felt but had never given a name.

How infuriating it was that a wad of branches and dirt had been more right about Mikal than he had been about himself.

But where had this mysterious story hidden deep inside Mikal come from? And how long had it been hiding there?

The first time Mikal had picked up an ink pen to write down his thoughts, his father had screamed at him for it. The pen—which Mikal had saved up a measure of rings to buy after working long days in the orchard—had been thrown onto the log fire.

Mikal had watched the golden flames eat the ink, the pen, and the soft feather on top. He had tried to block out his father's yelling as the man had sputtered that ink pens were for writing scriptures of the faith, and that was all. Not stories of nonsense. That Mikal would not grow to be a good, faithful folk if he did not do all he could to better himself in his *faith*.

How Mikal had hated that man for being such a hypocrite when the Ruby Legion came to the door seeking recruits one starry Winter night. Mikal had sworn during those seasons of his timestring that he would never be a scribe of the sacred truths or have anything to do with the things of the old faith.

But perhaps that day, watching his quill burn up in the fire, was when his true story had filled his heart. The one he had never written. The one he had never told. The one the forest had spotted and poked.

The Red Kingdom palace was dusted with snow, its scarlet banners rippling in the breeze. Mighty white pillars held the balconies in place, resembling the stone legs of strong, resilient giants. Everything a Ruby Legionnaire was meant to be.

Mikal abandoned the wagon in the Scarlet City and pulled the Green prince the rest of the way on foot with Redson guarding their backs. They marched through the garden of ice sculptures and over the courtyards, but their trio came to a halt when a toddler on wobbly legs wandered out from around a sculpture and cut off their path. Mikal blinked down at the boy with mahogany hair, burgundy eyes, and a silver coronet atop his head. The Migraithes were not certain whether they ought to bow.

The little Red Prince blinked up at Edward Green.

"Hi," the boy said, drawing a white apple from his velvet coat pocket. When he bit into it, it made a loud crunch. He did not break eye contact with the Green prince as he chewed, studying him all the while. The boy did not even have all his teeth yet.

A smile threatened the corner of Edward Green's mouth. "Hi," he said in return.

An ivory-haired woman swished out from the palace, and Mikal and Redson straightened their backs for the Crimson Queen.

The queen tugged the little Red Prince back. "Don't talk to him, Cane," she snapped. "He's a dead folk." Her icy glare fired up to the Green prince, and Mikal felt Edward flinch beneath his grip.

"Apologies, Your Majesty." Redson grabbed Edward Green's other shoulder and dragged him away from the royals, casting Mikal a look of worry.

When they entered the throne room in their muddy leather boots, high ranking members of the Crimson Court scowled at the Green prince, at the muddy trail they left on the floor, at the situation as a whole. Mikal knew he smelled of the forest. Not of the palace perfumes like the people here in claret robes.

Scarlet light flooded the white tile floor from the windows where the sun burned through. Nobles in long dresses and flowery holly wreaths watched with snoopy eyes and quiet whispers. Some of them had perhaps recognized the Migraithe brothers.

But *all* recognized Edward Green.

The king settled his purple eyes on the enemy prince with a smug smile.

"You will not escape me twice, Green. I will give you one last free choice before your timestring is snuffed out and you're given back to the snow from which you were made," the king decided, rising from his gilded seat. "You may choose which of the Legionnaires beside you to face in my arena at tomorrow's midday."

Mikal stilled. He had slain many of the Crimson King's enemies. But now he looked at Redson to read his brother's reaction.

Redson's face was stone, as it always was in the king's presence. He was a fit, obedient Legionnaire.

Everything Mikal was supposed to be in this moment.

Mikal's hand drifted down to the parchment-wrapped pen in his pocket, where he had inked a tale that this Green prince had recited back to him without knowing it.

"As I turned your father to snow, I shall turn you to snow," the king promised Edward Green. The king sent them off to lock Edward away with a nod. But as the Migraithe brothers left, the Crimson King slipped in one last word to the prince, "And in twenty plus five seasons, I shall claim your sister's life, too."

Beneath his grip, Mikal felt the Prince of the Pines go rigid.

The night felt colder than usual. Mikal rolled onto his side, basking in the moonlight spilling through the slated shutters of the Ruby Legion House. Redson lay awake, reading the newssheets and sipping a steaming cup of tea packed with healing herbs from the palace. It seemed he had already read through the Natter Nugget and was halfway through the articles of the Pebble Paper.

"If you want to ask me a question, brother, just ask it. You might be quiet, but your intentions speak louder than a howling polar bear." Redson did not even look up from the newssheets as he said it.

Mikal glided his fingers through his freshly washed hair. He had been pleased to see a full, steaming bath waiting for him upon arrival to his chambers. The palace attendants knew his tastes well. But he had been unsettled, even after he'd sank into the hot tub to ease his chilled bones.

"If we were not Legionnaires, what would we be, Redson?" Mikal rolled onto his back and fiddled with the tassels at the throat of his nightshirt.

"That's a riddlesome question." Redson dropped the Pebble Paper to his lap.

"Just answer it."

Redson released a sigh as he thought about it. "I suppose we would be apple farmers. We were good at that."

"We wouldn't. We would never have gone back to the orchards." Mikal dropped the tassels and glanced at his brother.

"Well. I suppose I might have become a teacher then," Redson admitted.

A slow, funny smile found Mikal's mouth. "Yes. I can imagine that."

"It's not because I like to tell everyone how to do everything," Redson clarified, and Mikal snorted, "it's because I think I would be good at explaining things to people eager to learn them." After a long sip of tea, Redson asked, "What about you, brother? If our souls had not been purchased by the Ruby Legion, what do you wish you could have been?" But he laughed before Mikal could answer. "Oh, I know. You'd be an Ink Whipper. You'd probably fill a dusty old library with a bunch of boring stories no one would ever read."

Mikal slid the remains of a biscuit off his night table and flung it at his brother. It slapped Redson in the eye, and Redson shrieked. Mikal was the one smiling now.

After a moment, Redson lifted his newssheets again. "Maybe we could be all those things. Scribes. Teachers. *And* Legionnaires."

Mikal's smile faded. Redson's did too. They went back to their own thoughts.

Mikal thought of the day he and his brother had sworn themselves on bended knee to the Crimson Crown. It was the day they had been informed that they would be Legionnaires, and Legionnaires only, until the day they took their last breath of cold Winter air.

FOURTHLY

The morning buzzed with energy as the Migraithe brothers marched the white hallways of the palace. The walls were gilded with the rising sun, the air filled with the scents of spices from the morning feast. Members of the Crimson Court who had scarcely cast the brothers a glance before nodded to them now as they made their way to the basement to collect their prisoner-prize.

Nobles and palace attendants alike whispered of the quarrel to take place between the Green prince and one of his captors. It seemed the prince had not yet chosen which of the Migraithe brothers he wished to face in the arena, but Mikal wished the prince would choose him so he might spare Redson from having to do it. Mikal did not care for the fame of bringing an enemy royal to his knees, though that was how most would see it if Mikal tried to sway the prince's choice his way.

So, as always, Mikal kept his mouth shut as they padded down the stairs in their leather palace slippers, glimmering in the shiniest copper armour the costume rooms of the Red Palace had to offer. They had been dressed and coached by the Directors of Tournaments before they headed to collect their prince. They had left their swords with the Directors to be cleaned and polished, too.

"Best of luck, brother. I imagine the prince will choose to fight you," Redson said as the cool dimness of the base-ment enveloped them. Mikal said nothing in response.

When they came to the dungeon cells, the smells in the air changed. Replacing the pleasant aromas of breakfast was the stale whiff of rot and despair. Mikal never enjoyed visit-ing this level of the palace. He had put a good measure of the prisoners in these cages himself.

The Prince of the Pines was huddled in the corner. He looked ill: white-faced, dry lips, sunken eyes of gold. It seemed it had been a chilly night in the dungeons.

"Ragnashuck, is he even alive?" Redson murmured.

At the question, the Green prince lifted his head, his gaze dragging over to the brothers. "I am quite alive. Yes."

"For now," Redson muttered, and the prince's jaw slid out.

Mikal drew out the key he had been handed by a rather pretty gray-eyed Director of Tournaments-in-training who had been at the morning meeting. He slid the key into the lock, the loud echo of it unlatching filling the dim dungeon.

The Green prince's gaze settled on the key for a moment.

"Out." It was all Mikal said as he slid the key into his pocket, out of sight.

The prince pulled himself off the floor and shivered as

he padded over the stone in his thick woodsman boots.

"They could have at least fed him," Redson grunted. "It's insulting to make one of us fight such a scrawny, sick thing. This won't be a challenge in the slightest."

Mikal ignored his brother's complaints and took the prince's collar to tug him out of the cell.

Redson filled the walk back upstairs with mindless nattering. He commented on the glances of the ladies they passed, the brightness of the sun in his eyes, the cleanliness of the recently scrubbed tile floors.

"You are blind," Edward Green whispered in the midst of it, and Mikal's gaze dragged over to the prince.

"You are a dead folk," Mikal pointed out with equal confidence. Their private conversation brought Redson's chatter to a stop, finally.

"No, you don't understand," the prince huffed, clasping his hands so tight, Mikal wondered how the wooden rings did not make it painful. "You could hear the forest," the prince said. "You are being *called* to something. And the longer you refuse to listen to it, the longer you will stay blind!"

They had halted in the hallway. Mikal and Edward were equals in height, but Edward was thin and flimsy, and Mikal, strong and deadly. The Green prince could see this well enough, yet still he looked back and forth between Mikal's eyes.

"But perhaps you already know this…" the prince said, realization trickling into the gold.

Someone approached, and Mikal swivelled the Green prince to keep walking before they were asked why they were standing around. Redson cast Mikal an odd look, perhaps asking what the prince was talking about.

It took several steps for Mikal to recognize that the female folk coming toward them was the same young Director of Tournaments-in-training who had been at the meeting that morning. The one who had handed him the key to Edward Green's cell.

It took another step for Mikal to realize that the girl's sharp, gray eyes had found the Green prince and that the Green prince, in return, was smiling.

But it took a measure too long for Mikal to notice the girl had slipped a key from her dress pocket and placed it into the lock of a door just a dip ahead.

Mikal was too slow in realizing a thing was not right.

When the door opened, a rush of cool air swept into the hall from the room—or was it a room? Mikal blinked at the opening through which he saw an angular space with a lit fire and walls of round stones and mortar.

The Green prince suddenly tore from Mikal's grip, fabric slipping against Mikal's nails. Redson bellowed in protest, but in the heartbeat it took them to realize what was happening, the prince sprang through the door along with the sharp-eyed Director of Tournaments, and the door began to swing closed behind them.

Redson reached the door before it latched, slamming it back open. He leapt through the opening, and as the memory of Redson being swallowed by the sinking hole in the forest filled Mikal's mind, Mikal followed before it was too late.

Mikal's fists slammed the ground to catch himself as he landed on the other side of the door. The ground was cold and not like the palace at all. The sound of a door clicking shut behind him filled his ears. He spun to find the girl with gray eyes, her hand pressed flat against the door, and the glow of lanterns lighting half her face.

Most of the room was warmed with the liquid light, and as Mikal turned to see where he was, his face fell. For, before him and his brother stood a modest army of ten. Edward Green was among them, and the musical fellow they had crossed in the forest was with them, too: Charlie Little.

Redson glanced to Mikal as if to ask what they should do. The brothers remained on their knees before this group. Mikal's hand went to his belt in search of a sword that was not there.

"Legionnaires." The girl from the palace spoke. Mikal tried his best to recall her name. It had been spoken a time or three at the meeting. A large ring with keys of all sizes and colours hung from her belt, making a metallic song as she came to stand in front of them. "We've found ourselves in quite the muddle," she said.

Past her, Edward Green was led away by the muscular, purple-winged fairy Mikal remembered from the snow fields. The fairy pulled out a loaf of spiced bread and mumbled to Edward that he should eat.

Mikal's gaze flicked back to the girl. "Cora," he blurted as the name came back to him. "Do you think my brother and I cannot escape your little magic trick? You are not safe from us, not even here. We have no intention of letting you get away with stealing our prince. And if you knew what we are capable of, you'd run from us as fast as your legs can carry you." It was the greatest measure of words he had spoken at once in a long time. "You're a master of keys," he added. "I suppose I should have guessed a Guardian of

Doors was aiding the Green prince all this time. It explains a thing or three."

"I am not a Guardian of Doors. I am not ancient, nor as powerful as that. And I do not have to answer your questions, Legionnaire. Especially not *here*."

Mikal stole another look around as if to ask where *here* was.

"Room Four Hundred Plus Six," Redson answered. The girl's gaze whipped toward Redson who nodded up to the sign on the wall where a lengthy poem was written:

The Objective
Of Room Four Hundred Plus Six

Show love to the Rime Folk
Feed the poorest
Heal the sick
Shelter the orphans
Provide for the widows
Preach the merry news of Truth

And above all, know and believe that
Elowin is King of all Winter Kings
And Lord of all Winter Lords

Redson's grunt spoiled the silence. "Who wrote that preposterous creed?"

But Mikal's mouth had gone dry. "I did," he whispered.

With a shaking hand, Mikal reached for his pocket where a story in ink was hidden away. He drew out his pen and unwrapped the parchment to see if it was true—if perhaps his memory was deceiving him. When he unrolled it, Redson leaned to read over his shoulder, and the word that came from Redson next said it all:

"Ragnashuck."

Mikal's whisper filled the quiet room, "I have been writing my own story all along," he said.

Once upon a Winter's snow
A crushed Rime soul began to grow
With a hard spirit and a heart of anger
He cast his hate at every stranger

Gifted, he was, in scribing tales of the stars
But he used his gift to bring upon scars
He served the darkness because he was blind
But soon he would see all he'd left behind

Upon the Winter's snow one sweet morning
He would meet a merry band who would sing:

"Show love to the Rime Folk
Feed the poorest of all
Heal those who are sick

Catch the orphans before they fall
Provide aid to the widows
And preach the merry news
But what is most important
Is one's belief in the Truth"

Mikal let the parchment fall to the floor of Room Four Hundred Plus Six. "We have been blind."

Redson's buttery gaze dropped to Mikal's shaking hands. "What are your fingers doing, brother?" he asked. "Are you ill?"

It was then Mikal glanced down at where his hand was curled, his fingers pinched as though something was meant to be between them, and he performed small, graceful strokes into the air.

"Pinespittle," Charlie Little said in his melodic voice from where he stood at Cora's side. "He's writing."

Mikal took hold of his wrist with his other hand to force it still, but he could not seem to stop the story trying to be written. The story that would not go quiet. The story that would not let him ignore it any longer. The story that he had been telling all along, that would now find its ending.

When Mikal looked at his brother, something changed. Redson stood straight, and a moment later he shouted to those in the room, "Get my brother an ink pen and some parchment!"

LASTLY, AND SO FORTH

Mikal Migraithe, the Ink Whipper, listened to the stories of the skies of Winter, the tales of old trees, and the sweet, praising hollers below the snow. Mikal's heart filled with verses as he listened to the accounts. When he began, he found he could not stop writing until Room Four Hundred Plus Six was overflowing with manuscripts. Redson took it upon himself to bind the pages into books, and when the number of volumes became too great, they sought out a network of ice caves outside the Red Kingdom. They stored the books there, along with all the Volumes of Wisdom originals scribed by prophets and Ink Whippers of ages past.

The Ruby Legion tried to find the vanished elite hunters for quarters to come. But the Crimson King soon forgot about the Migraithes, for he was fixated on the Prince of the Pines who had escaped him a time again with no explanation and not a witness to speak of where he had gone.

The Migraithe brothers never went back for their swords, their weapons, and their brutal seasons of hunting.

But on a cool Winter's day, when a band of humble snow shepherds passed by the ice caves with a flock, the brothers traded a night of storytelling for a pair of old, weathered cane-topped staffs.

And it was with those staffs their true journey began.

This is the account of the Migraithe brothers who were once worth less than a pocket full of rings.

Who were once lost but then were found again.

Who were blind but were made to see.

THE

CORD

A

DOZEN

STRANDS

Novella, The Fourth

FIRSTLY

Cora

Cora Thimble had not been a typical Rime child. Upon birth, she had peered around with the clear, silver gaze of a babe and had seen the world differently than the other Red King-dom children. She had been gifted with dreams and had al-ways carried the most unexplainable adoration for different shades of metal, as was reflected in the sheen of her sharp, iron-like eyes.

The fair-featured girl had learned to run before the other sputtlepuns in the earliest seasons of her timestring. She had not waited for the others to catch up. She had chased the horizon, chased her dreams, and she had chased the quiet, soothing whispers in the night to discover what they were saying.

And what she learned from her travels, from her dreams, and from the whispers, was a thing not commonly spoken of in the Red Kingdom.

For, Cora Thimble had come to know the Voice of Truth itself. And for many seasons, she sought him out, never being able to put a face to the voice until the eve she stumbled into the hidden library by accident and came face-to-face with the one who called himself *Elowin*.

It was the same eve she met Charlie.

The torch flickered by Cora's face as she rushed down the alleyway of stones glimmering from icy raindrops. The storm would cause her light to sputter out soon. She tugged the hood of her cloak a pinch further over her eyes, scanning the dim cobbled street for signs of watching evil. She rounded the tea rooms, inhaling the scents of medicinal herbs and black powders, and joined in the thick crowd of moving folk, all pushing in different directions through the heart of the Scarlet City. Her gaze worked its way around the public square even when the rest of her body walked straight. She studied faces, name tags, cloaks, and hoods. She studied corners and cracks and every other unusual place she passed.

Ahead, a set of flaming blue eyes peeked out from beneath a hood similar to her own. Cora locked gazes with the folk as he came her way. She slid a rolled piece of parchment from her pocket and held it at her side.

A simple inquiry was scribed upon the slip in Mikal's handwriting:

We're searching for Juniper Strenson and Wade Pan who have gone missing from our numbers.
Please send any information you can find.

In a flit of seconds, the blue-eyed sputtlepun passed, brushing her arm, and the message was delivered. Cora returned her hand to her empty pocket and tossed the torch, now only half lit, into the snow at the roadside where it snuffed out.

She inhaled the night, breathing in the cool, frosted air, and made for the Red Kingdom palace where she would soon be expected.

A curious eye turned her way. A Ruby Legionnaire and his partner stood at the end of the square where the cobbled streets turned to onyx. Cora halted, drawing the Legionnaires to study her further.

She turned for the next alley instead—a narrow thing hardly wide enough for her body—and she squeezed through to the other side where a band of Red elves played flutes and rattled silver bells. A modest audience tossed rings into their baskets.

Cora slipped into the crowd, tugging a gold ring from her pocket and dropping it into the nearest basket. She stepped back into the clapping folk, blending into the tallest ones' shadows. Through the crowd's cracks, Cora spotted the Legionnaires squeeze through the alley. They looked this way and that, murmuring a thing or three, and they split up to scour the street.

Cora spun around a couple in matching claret head-dresses and slipped back into the narrow alley, glancing over her shoulder as she did. But when she brought her gray eyes ahead, she stopped mid-step.

Waiting at the end of the alley were ten plus four Legionnaires. Very likely searching for a sputtlepun girl in a black cloak such as hers. The sputtlepun girl drawn on advertisements of warning and posted around the Scarlet City this last quarter.

She sprang for the town square, ducking around a golden reindeer-drawn sleigh. The deer almost trampled the first Legionnaire who leapt after her. Cora's chest pumped as all ten plus four Legionnaires gave chase. She was slight, but not strong; she would never break free if they caught her.

Cora flitted past a bouquet of sparkling white flowers and ducked beneath a crimson banner with the royal crest. The rain turned heavy, transforming into bulbs of ice that bounced over the black streets. The noise covered her panting as she slid around the Cider House and was captured by a pair of strong hands.

She and her captor spun once around on the ice-covered street, their feet flat, their balance perfect because they had each other. Cora would have shrieked had he not been so warm, and had he not held her in such a promising way. Charlie Little had a puzzled face when he glanced past her toward the road, his fingers tightening around her elbow.

"I need to be at the palace, or they'll realize I'm a part of this, Charlie," Cora whispered.

Charlie nodded, drawing his gaze back to her as he unfastened her cloak. "Let me deal with this," he said, tugging the cloak from her shoulders and draping it around himself.

When he drew up the hood, Cora could hardly see his face anymore in the shadow. She opened her mouth to remind him he would not be spared if he was caught.

But in the dimness, Charlie smiled. Flattered, likely, that she appeared concerned.

"Get to the palace," he said a time again. "I'll see you

soon."

Without another word, Charlie raced over the ice in his thick forest boots. Cora watched him go for a moment before she turned and walked up the roadside as slowly as she could manage with her heart slamming against her chest.

The Ruby Legionnaires flew around the corner with shouts, and Cora swallowed, fighting to keep her eyes ahead.

She could not turn back for Charlie.

She could not look back at Charlie.

She could not do anything for Charlie.

She could only keep walking forward as though she had nothing to hide.

Cora came in the palace side doors hoping to draw less attention, but her wet slippers slapped over the floor, alerting those standing by. Most ignored her and went back to their duties. But one member of the Crimson Court fixed his eyes upon her and dropped his scrolls to the nearest table.

His name was engraved on a golden nameplate always fixed over his heart:

Sullen Sprit-Spellborrow

"Miss Thimble," he said, coming before her with a speck of worry on his brow as he took in her sopping wet clothes, shivering hands, bluing skin, and messy hair. "Have you been hurt?"

"No." Cora tried to form a smile, but her cheeks were too cold to work. "I lost my cloak in the city and had to race back before I froze. That's all."

Sullen eyed her as he nodded. "Of course. I'll have an attendant send tea to your chambers immediately." The young scribe had his black hair smooth and neat this eve. Ready for the tournament, it seemed. His wild yellow gaze made Cora drop her own eyes to the tiled floor.

"Thank you," she said before brushing past him and scurrying up the stairs toward her chambers.

"Miss Thimble?" Sullen's voice carried up the stairs and Cora slowed. When she turned, she tried a time again to raise that smile, but could not. Sullen's unusual eyes took her in as she stood there. "Next time you go wandering out into the Winter dark, bring a spare cloak."

The suggestion should have been innocent, but Cora felt it crawl down her spine. She nodded, and Sullen drifted back to the table to collect his scrolls. Only when he wandered down the hall and disappeared did Cora find the strength to move again.

She released a breath when she turned, and she scurried the rest of the way up the stairs to her room.

The soft echo of roars flitted through the palace. Cora imagined the spectators in the arena tossing plums and waving scarlet flags.

There was no time for a bath. She tore her drenched dress away and replaced it with another, checking the glass clock on the wall.

Cora wrapped herself in a sparkling, gold organza overskirt and a ruby-covered bodice. She brushed golden powders over her eyelids and smeared red paint on her lips then hopped over to check the mirror when she was finished. She strutted for the door, snatching her nameplate on her way, and lacing her most valuable rings onto her fingers. But she paused, hand on the knob. She glanced back at her room when she realized she did not have her keys.

"By the sharpest wind," she muttered as she pictured her key ring still in the pocket of the cloak Charlie wore. She flattened her palm against her forehead and yanked the door open, fluttering from her room and rushing toward the arena.

The Crimson Court didn't notice her sweep in through the back doors of the observatory. They exchanged whispers and lifted drinks to their painted lips, batting their long lashes at each other and twirling cherry garland around their fingers as they waited to be entertained. Cora slid around them, scanning the balcony for the rest of the Directors of Tournaments. But she stopped when she reached the balcony's rail.

The Directors of Tournaments were not here.

"Feast your eyes!" An announcer's voice rattled the room, and Cora jumped. She looked into the pit of the arena and blanched. For, there were the Directors of Tournaments, stationed in a line for all to see. And she was not with them.

"Miss Thimble, are you not meant to be down there?" Lady Yemma inquired from her seat. Cora turned to the aged woman in time to see Sullen Sprit-Spellborrow arrive at the back of the observatory. Lady Yemma's question had drawn his attention, and his eyes locked with Cora's.

"Yes." Cora dropped her gaze and slipped back through the balcony seats.

She descended the viewers' stairs and raced to the lowest level tunnels. She made it to the arena's stage just as the

Directors of Tournaments were leaving to the music of the spectators clapping. But Cora sprang back into the shadow of a pillar as the Directors exited the stage and moved through the tunnel, nattering quietly amongst themselves in their gold capes and rose-red jackets. She had missed an important moment. She did not want to think about what the Directors of Tournaments would do to her once they realized.

She exhaled and closed her eyes, leaning back against the cool pillar to ease the heat in her skin. She would have to craft an ashworm-worthy excuse.

When the voices in the tunnel ceased, Cora lifted from the pillar to make her way back, wiping a bead of sweat from her brow. She felt something brush her arm.

Cora gasped and spun around.

The tunnel appeared empty, the cheers of the spectators sifting through the space. Her gaze flickered to the shadowed corners, but not a thing moved.

"Cora."

She nearly screamed when she spun back around, but she bit her tongue.

There stood Sullen. An ink pen was in his hand, but his arms were folded. He tapped the pen against his bicep.

"What do you want?" she blurted, then slammed her mouth shut.

Sullen was covered in shadow, and Cora glided back a step.

"I don't think the Directors are very pleased with you." His pen tapping created an off-beat music that made Cora cringe. "I can speak to them for you," he offered. "I can tell the Directors about how you lost your cloak in the city and found yourself in a muddle. They won't care for the excuse, but it might sound better coming from a respected scribe."

"I don't need your help. I'll tell the Directors myself," Cora insisted. She tried to step around him, but Sullen drifted into her way.

"I know someone who can help you," he added. "Someone the Directors will listen to. Let me in, Cora."

"Don't use my first name," she warned, finally lifting her slicing stare to meet his. "We are not friends, Mr. Spellborrow."

The scribe frowned. His yellow gaze was potent, and Cora felt the urge to drop her eyes again. But she had seen how his powerful words could mindsweep a soul. She wanted him to know she would *not* accept his way of fixing things.

"Be careful," he warned. "Or the Crimson Court might start to think you ungrateful for all their charity." The words were laced with ice, and Cora felt them whisper across her flesh, right down to her fingertips. Her hand drifted toward her dress pocket for a set of keys she wouldn't find there.

But Sullen turned and sauntered out of the tunnel.

Cora's hand drifted up to her chest. "Elowin," she whispered. "Have they discovered me?" The prayer was small and quiet, and perhaps drowned out by the cheer that erupted from the spectators.

Cora did not hear a reply. She heard only the chants for death at her back.

She lifted her chin and walked from the tunnel, preparing a speech for the Directors of Tournaments who would have returned to the observatory balcony by now. And for the first time since Elowin had tasked her with birthing the underground cathedral, Cora wondered where Elowin was.

Elowin had not shown himself since the day he commissioned her and Charlie to start the church of the Red Kingdom. And each day that passed, Cora could feel something growing heavier, darker, and more monstrous. On cold nights, she was sure she could hear low growls of something sinister roaming beneath the kingdom, casting curses into the air, and drawing the proud to his offering of power.

SECONDLY

Charlie

Charlie Little slipped into the forest and nearly ran into Frosty's gaping, open mouth. He released the sort of high-pitched scream he was certain not even a lady could muster. Legionnaires filled the trees, but they were hardly as frightening as Frosty's icicle teeth and blizzard breath.

Between moments of fighting the Legionnaires and scaring the rest off, Frosty laughed; a deep, rumbling bellow that made Charlie scowl.

"Don't tell a soul I screamed like that!" he warned the not-snowsquatch as he waited for the folk in red capes to disperse.

When the forest was cleared of enemies, Charlie slid Cora's cloak from his shoulders. A light metallic clapping sound rose from within its pockets. He dove his hand into the fabric.

"By the sharpest wind," he breathed, a tune of concern dipping into his musical heart.

He had sent Cora to the palace alone, and for the first time since Charlie had known her, she did not have her keys. The girl who could disappear would be trapped.

Charlie took off running for the inn. "I'll see you later!" he sang back to Frosty without explaining himself. He ignored the howls of the wind over the trees and the rhythms of the clapping leaves above. They sang a song of war—a song of worry. They warned him to slow down, perhaps.

Charlie slid over the ice on flat boots and collided with the brittle door of Room Four Hundred Plus Six. The bang filled the street, and to his dismay, the door dislodged from its place and tumbled to the ground in three large pieces.

"Pinespittle," he mumbled, dropping to pick up one of the shards.

"What did you do to the frostbitten door?!" Redson Migraithe's question was nearly as loud as Charlie's collision had been, and Charlie shoved him back into Room Four Hundred Plus Six. He realized a long shard was still in his hand when he accidentally banged it against the table and spilled the pot of tea.

"Ragnashuck, you're a peg out of its shell, Little." Redson folded his arms. He did not try to help, he just watched.

"At least offer the peg a hand, brother." Mikal surveyed the scene as he entered: spilled tea, a broken door, a plank of wood in Charlie's hand. He reached to take the plank away from Charlie first.

"Quiet, spinbugs! You're going to get us discovered!" Edward rushed in from the hall and stopped before the gaping doorway. Worry overtook his gold eyes. "Shall I get the

Inn Keeper?"

"Don't trouble the Inn Keeper. He's done us service enough." Redson finally moved to gather the other pieces of the door still outside. "My brother and I will fix it. Don't muddy your hands, *Prince*."

Edward bristled and Mikal smirked.

"Has Cora come back?" Charlie cut in.

"Not yet, and neither has Angel. She's out looking for Juniper and Wade," Redson explained. "I'm worried about them after all that whipsteaming in the Pebble Papers. Some-one needs to stop Spellborrow from nattering those back-wards riddles."

"I'm not worried about Sullen Sprit-Spellborrow." Charlie grabbed a towel to clean the tea off the floor.

"Well, you should be. He's got eyes for Cora." Redson hauled the last shard of the door inside, but Charlie had gone still. Tea inched across the towel, soaking up to his fingers. He left it there—towel and all—and he stood, turning toward the Migraithe twins with new eyes.

"What did you just say?" he asked. The music of the simmering fireplace twisted.

"Ragnashuck, you really didn't know? Why do you think I suggested she have a word with him about his arti-cles? If anyone can sway him into tossing away his pen, it's her."

"Hush, Redson. You've made your point." Mikal looked across the room at Charlie, seeming to realize that, *no*, Char-lie did *not* know of the infamous scribe's feelings.

"And she's…" Charlie swallowed as the organ of wind outside burst into a crazed song. "…she's *trapped* in the pal-ace with him?"

171

"What do you mean?" Edward asked. "Charlie, why is Cora trapped?"

Charlie's fingers dove into the pocket of Cora's cloak, and he drew out the multi-toned set of metal keys clinging to one large brass ring.

THIRDLY

Cora

Cora hadn't the strength to return to the balcony. She did not come up with an appropriate excuse for the Directors, and even though she knew it would make matters worse, she avoided the arena altogether. She returned to her room, climbed into bed, and released a loud cough or three. When an attendant finally came to check on her, Cora feigned being ill. The Crimson Court had already seen her at the Tournament, and Sullen had already seen her in the tunnel, but she had to believe there was still a way out of this.

A knock sounded on the door, and Cora scrambled out of bed, wrapping herself in her bedside coat. She paused before she answered, pinching her nose roughly and stifling a croak at her own work as her nose burned in reaction.

She swung the door wide, presenting herself as the poor, little, sick Director-of-Tournaments-in-training who should be pitied… with a rather convincing red nose.

But her stomach dropped when Sullen's yellow eyes fixed on her beside coat, beneath which the hem of her golden dress sprouted at the floor. The handle of a cart rested beneath Sullen's fingers. He had brought tea and butternut squares. Once, those treats had been her favourite.

"I bring a peace offering," he said, taking his gaze off her ridiculous bedside coat and placing it on her face. "And I came to warn you that, as I suspected, the Court isn't pleased with you. I imagine some bad tidings are coming your way, Miss Thimble."

Cora felt her Rime blood turn warm. She knew that deep within her chest, colours of all sorts had turned bright and vibrant in her seasons. But they melted to knots now—the emerald mixing with the topaz, which bled into the amethyst. It was unusual to be aware that there were colours in one's chest, but Cora had always known it, just as she had always known that she did not belong at Sullen's side.

"I suppose I should invite you in," Cora said, reluctantly stepping aside.

Sullen rolled the cart into her room, eyeing the mess; particularly the trays of mismatched keys of all different sizes littering the room's surfaces. He stopped the cart by the fireplace and rounded it to pour some tea. With a steaming cup in his hand, he returned to Cora.

"To help make you *well* again," he said, passing it to her. His tone was cruel, almost a mockery of her pink nose and unconvincing bedside coat. But his lips spread into a closed-mouth smile.

Cora said nothing as she received the tea.

Sullen prepared himself a cup next. "I do not like to be

rejected, Cora." He got right to the point, and Cora froze with the cup a pinch from her lips. Sullen's yellow eyes flickered up. "And I do not offer help to many folk. When I do, I expect it to be received with gratitude."

Cora lowered the tea. She imagined splashing its contents into Sullen's proud eyes. "Then thank you for offering. I still do not accept. Though it is riddlesome why you should care so much."

Sullen's hands slowed as he poured the tea. "Is it?"

Cora no longer had an appetite.

"You should point your interest elsewhere, Sullen. I may never be a Director of Tournaments after my tardiness today." Cora forced herself to take a long, deep sip of tea. It tasted of chalky black powder, unsweetened by syrup. She wished to spit it out.

"You will be if I speak to the Directors about you. I have more influence in this palace than you think."

Though it was an offer, Cora only heard a threat.

"I cannot figure out your angle," she admitted, setting the cup back on the cart once and for all.

"And I cannot figure out yours." Sullen turned to face her, abandoning his tea as well. "You have one of the most coveted jobs in the Red Kingdom. You have power, beauty, and cunning. You have everything. Yet you're distracted, and I cannot figure out why."

Cora's fingers traced over her skirts where her empty pockets were, all covered up by her bedside coat.

"Let me settle your matters. Allow me to speak to the Directors on your behalf. I don't want a binding deal because I want nothing in return. I simply want you to let me *in*." Sullen's gaze was penetrating now.

"*In*, how?" Cora whispered. Her hands grew cold as she worked over the soft fabric. She slid them into her coat pockets as Sullen let out a long, heavy breath.

"I wish to introduce you to a new way of thinking that you have perhaps not tried before. I wish for you to see a thing or three...*differently*."

"A new way of thinking? Like the way you try to sway the Red Kingdom with your publications?" Cora challenged, and Sullen's face changed.

"What is wrong with my publications?"

Cora slammed her mouth shut, realizing she had said a thing too soon.

Sullen tilted his head and drew in a step so his breath warmed her face when he spoke, "What is wrong with my publications, Cora?" he asked again.

"Nothing." Cora dropped her gaze back to her palace slippers. She shook her head, wishing she could take it back. "Nothing at all, Sullen. I'm feeling ill and my thoughts are muddled. Forgive me."

Sullen did not speak right away. After a moment, he turned and took the handle of the cart. "You will not gain the forgiveness of the Directors without me," he assured. "Think on it, Cora. I am your best chance at keeping your power."

A pinch later, he was rolling the cart out the door of her room. Cora did not move a muscle until he was gone.

The windows blazed with scarlet sunlight, tearing through the stained glass and casting geometric shapes upon the white palace walls in the morning. Cora strutted through the hall to the meeting of the Crimson Court, the buzzing of truthspire still warming her tongue. She hoped she was not asked a question, or even looked at by anyone, until the meeting was over.

In the grand meeting room, starlight-chandeliers dangled from the ceiling heights, and glorious paintings by revered Red Kingdom artists covered the walls. The magnificent window was recently polished and glistening.

The Crimson Court was abuzz. Velvety red lips relayed secrets and gossip, and square necklines were paired with black pearl necklaces purchased from the snowseas divers. In the corner the scribes gathered, chatting quietly amongst themselves. One of them had long diamond-white hair all the way to his waist. Cora could not remember the fellow's name.

Sullen turned from the group and caught her eye as though he knew the very moment she had set foot into the meeting room.

Cora made her way to her seat. Her hair was twisted into a braid, her nails painted silver, her eyelids dusted with rose-gold. She was well-suited today to play her part. She would fool this court and make up for her terrible misstep from the eve prior. She had a convincing story to tell of where she had been, one that even Sullen might believe.

The natter in the room dropped to whispers as the Crimson King marched up the dais stairs. He wore his full suit of copper armour, as did the young Red Princes who followed him. The burgundy-haired prince licked a sugary bubblebaker.

The king did not waste any time addressing his court. "A

measure of my Legionairres were attacked in the woods yesternight by an *abomination* of a snowsquatch. It was said to have looked like something horrid from the ancient spell books."

Cora chewed on her lip. She would have laughed at the king's description of the not-snowsquatch, had she not been sitting among the court. She hoped that if the Ruby Legion had crossed Frosty it meant Charlie had gotten away safely.

The king's voice crackled like a fire. "I want that thing hunted and destroyed so everything out there like it remembers never to cross the Legion. And, *kingsblood*, I want that frostbitten Green prince found! I am now offering seven hundred plus fifty gold rings for his capture."

Gasps lifted through the room and a flit of fear met Cora's stomach. A reward like that would put the whole kingdom on high alert. People would turn mad, tearing apart their neighbours' homes and marching the streets with weapons to hunt for Edward.

The Crimson King made other announcements of less important things, but Cora thought only of the reward. Perhaps she should warn Edward. Perhaps he should run for the hills before the Red Kingdom lost control.

The Crimson Court laughed as a group of folk with bound wrists were led to the stage alongside the king. Cora's attention lifted to study the faces through the thickly splattered red paint. Her heart stopped.

"Juniper…" She whispered the name before she could stop it from slipping out. Six criminals lined the stage, recently arrested in the Scarlet City for petty crimes. Cora blinked away moisture as she took in the two folk at the end.

Juniper Strenson and Wade Pan, two members of Cora

Thimble's underground cathedral. Two partners of Cora's and Charlie's. Two of the *ten plus two* who made up Elowin's Cord of a Dozen Strands. Two who had gone to great lengths these quarters past to help grow the cathedral and spread the merry news of the True King's arrival.

They had been here, prisoners in the Red Kingdom palace.

Juniper blinked paint from her eyes as she studied the faces in the room. When she found Cora, Cora looked away, a sting entering her gut for doing so, but knowing that if anyone saw them exchange a look it would be her demise, and Juniper and Wade's as well.

Cora's fingers traced over her empty pockets.

She had to get them out.

Juniper and Wade needed to escape the palace before it was too late.

FOURTHLY

Cora

Cora had been forced to turn her back to her friends. She had been forced to walk out of the meeting room with her chin up and her eyes hard. And she had been forced to leave the palace again, instead of smoothing things over with the Directors of Tournaments.

The rain had returned. The hike through the city had been unbearable in her thin burgundy palace cloak. Cora checked over her shoulder as she rounded the fountain to the Inn and came to knock against the door of Room Four Hundred Plus Six. She made a face when she realized the door had changed. A messy plate of patched up scraps was where the door was supposed to be.

When it cracked open a pinch, a ridiculous smile appeared on the other side. "Are you selling something?" he asked.

Cora sighed. "Open the door, Charlie. I'm drenched."

"Ah. That you are." Charlie took in her saturated cloak. "Tea, then." But his smile faded as she came in. In his eyes, she saw worry. Charlie opened his mouth, but after a moment of not quite deciding what to say, he stopped trying and closed it again.

Cora hung her dripping cloak on the hooks by the door and inhaled the lovely aroma of spiced tea. It seemed Mikal had steeped a pot recently. Cora imagined the Ink Whipper sipping it in some corner while hunched over a desk, scribbling verses. The thought brought her comfort.

She turned to find Charlie holding out a steaming mug. She sighed in relief and took it in her cold fingers. Cora had craved Mikal's spiced tea since sipping that awful chalky flavour Sullen had mixed.

"I almost came to the palace to see if you were all right," Charlie admitted quite suddenly. It seemed that was what he had settled upon to say.

"I was fine, Charlie," Cora promised, though her hand brushed along her pocket. "Do you have my keys?"

Charlie pulled them out as if he could not wait to be rid of them, and he handed them over.

Cora's fingers traced over the familiar brass ring and each key with its specific purpose. She slid the whole lot of them into her dress, swearing to never lose them again.

"I did not actually come for my keys," she admitted. "I came because of Juniper and Wade."

"Angel hasn't returned yet with any news of them," Charlie said. "We've all been stuck here listening to Redson natter while we wait." He drifted back to the table and poured himself a cup of tea.

Cora made a face. "Make him wear a muzzle," she suggested, and Charlie burst out laughing, knocking the handle of the teapot. It tumbled off balance and fell to the floor with a thud, spilling its contents over the hardwood.

Charlie scowled. "Not again," he moaned.

A loud knock sounded on the door, and Cora's smile fell. She and Charlie traded a gaze before she swept around to open it. Every time someone knocked, those inside hushed with the same thoughts. Cora's hand slid into her pocket, reminding herself she had her keys back, and that the Hall of Doors was only a short sprint down the hall. She opened the door.

A girl stood outside, her hood dripping with rain as Cora's had been.

"It's Angel," Cora said, then swung the door wide.

The girl marched in and dropped a satchel on the table. Cora sealed the door shut, silencing the storm which had changed from heavy rainfall to the sprinkling of ice pellets again.

Angel unfastened her cloak and tossed it onto the hooks beside Cora's, revealing the girl's long blue-black hair and the shimmering silver tattoos circling her tanned neck.

"You're back." Redson Migraithe appeared in the arch, leaning against the frame. He cast Angel a sweet smile.

"I got supplies," Angel said, nodding to the satchel. "Food. And parchment for your brother. I imagine he's a scribble away from running out."

"Awe, how thoughtful." Redson smiled again.

Charlie cleared his throat, and Cora stifled a smile. Angel and Redson either hated or admired each other on any given day. It changed by the hour, but it seemed this eve they were getting along just fine.

"And I brought the newssheets, like you asked." Angel dug into her pocket and withdrew a rolled up, damp leaflet of paper. "But they say nothing of Juniper and Wade. Perhaps our friends had to hide for a measure so they wouldn't be caught."

Cora's smile faded. "I already found them," she said, and all eyes turned her way. "I found them while I was at the palace. It's why I came back."

A cold silence hung in the air until Redson muttered, "Ragnashuck."

Cora hugged her arms to herself. "I have to get them out. We know what will happen if we leave them there." She closed her eyes and rubbed her temples. Her secret was holding together by a single red thread.

"Cora..." Charlie's voice was small. He seemed to be thinking the same thing.

Redson took the leaflet from Angel and flipped it open. "Is there anything in the Pebble Paper about them?"

"Why do you read those, Redson?" Cora asked. "We've been at this for three quarters and those newssheets are only getting less and less uplifting."

"Speaking of *uplifting*..." Redson adjusted his stance and folded his arms. "You know I believe Elowin is real and who you say he is, right?" he said, and Cora heard the strain in the once-Legionnaire's question. "But why hasn't he shown himself to me and Mikal? We have been faithfully serving as part of the Cord of a Dozen Strands for three full quarters. And still, he has not shown himself to us. Why do you suppose that is?"

Cora felt Charlie's eyes upon her, perhaps asking the

same question. "Maybe you're not ready," she offered. Truthfully, she did not know the reason Elowin did not show himself to the entire dozen. It made it difficult to keep up the faith when all had not yet seen the face of the True King of Winter. Apart from Cora, Charlie, and the fairy who often checked in on Edward, Elowin had not revealed himself to anyone else. The group had been forced to take Cora's and Charlie's word for it.

Redson did not seem convinced by her guess.

"We are Elowin's dozen," she reminded them. "The ten plus two who have built this underground cathedral, which will act as every faculty of ministry. As a body needs hands, feet, a head, and a heart, so does a church need different minds and gifts. Elowin has given us this task, and we will walk by faith, even when we cannot see him."

Redson's gaze flickered to the wall, but he nodded. "Yes. I suppose I knew what we were getting ourselves into when we abandoned the Legion. I just thought he would have shown himself by now."

Angel tapped over the wood floors in her wet boots and took the leaflet back from Redson. "Perhaps we should be done with these newssheets. We can check them for news of our captured friends, but Cora is right; these articles are only getting worse. The Pebble Paper claims we're a threat, following the ideals of an old religion that no longer has breath. And their witch—that young girl who slays their enemies in their arena—she has a strange darkness in her. I've seen her fight. She's not quite right in the head."

"It's the blackness," Cora said. "I can feel it, especially in the palace. I can hear it uttering curses upon this kingdom on a silent night. I know it's the opposite of Elowin's light.

It's a Beast hiding below the Red Kingdom, pacing in its den, waiting to devour the Rime Folk above. That's why I cannot leave my post in the palace until I discover what it is."

"Cora," Charlie objected again, his boots dragging over the hardwood to meet her. "We should wait for Elowin to show himself again before you go back. You can't keep taking this risk."

"I'm going back, Green. I've survived a good measure of seasons in that palace, and I'll survive this too."

Charlie did not say anything else.

Edward walked in eating a ginger snap. He was followed by Mikal, Ribble Tuff, Jerry Jinglefoot, and John Dough, who carried in a steaming pan of gingerbread cookies.

"Haid," Cora said to the Green prince, who paused his munching. "The Crimson King has put a large bounty on your head. It won't be safe for you to stay here much longer."

Edward set his half-eaten ginger cookie back on the tray, drawing a grimace from John Dough. "It has never been safe for me here, Red."

"This is different. You're important."

"We're *all* important—"

"You may have to leave for a pinch," Cora said firmly. "I won't let the Crimson King have the true heir to the Green Kingdom throne. You don't realize what he'll do to you if he finds you." Her gaze slid to the others in their company.

"What would you have us do, Thimble?" Ribble Tuff asked, scratching at the large curly bun of hair atop his head.

"We need to be cunning these next days. I can feel a thing changing," she said.

"As can I," Mikal agreed.

"Me too." It was Charlie who said it last.

Cora nodded. "Then let us be as clever as ashworms, and as careful as pegs. Because if we make one mistake now, we'll all be turned to snow."

FIFTHLY

Redson

Redson Migraithe had not been as angry of a boy as his brother in the early seasons of their timestrings. But that was only because when Redson spoke aloud, his own words brought him comfort. There was a release of peace in saying a thing or three, in putting feelings and thoughts into the air. It left little mystery to worry about between comrades. It let one share their troubles with others, and therefore share their burdens too. While Mikal had soothed his own soul with his storytelling and writing, Redson had dealt with the bruises on his dusty Rime heart by speaking his thoughts and letting them live on in others.

But for all his nattering, the one thing Redson had not been able to utter yet was how he felt about Angel Snow.

The youthful warrior was an orphan who *claimed* to

have been raised by fairies. It was all very fascinating. Redson considered this as the girl of his thoughts came into the living space of Room Four Hundred Plus Six and lifted a log onto the fire to keep the flames alive.

"Where did you say you grew up again, Snow?" Redson asked, hoping that just once she would slip up and tell him her truths.

But the corner of Angel's mouth turned up. "I did not tell you. And I never will."

Redson sat down on the velvet sofa he and Mikal had dragged all the way to this room from the nearest village. It was not the most comfortable thing, but it kept the Cord happy to be able to sit together.

"You said you grew up on an island," he pressed, folding his hands.

Angel rearranged the fire with the metal poker and released a laugh. "I did say that," she realized. "Your skills of interrogation are serving you well, Legionnaire."

Redson released a proud grunt. "That they are."

Angel finished with the fire and drew her dual-bladed sword from where it had been leaning on the wall. She pulled out a cloth to clean it, scrubbing at the metal. Her gaze flickered up to him though, catching him still watching. Waiting for an answer.

Finally, she joined Redson in the sitting area. Her silver neck tattoos sparkled against the light of the lively fire. She never spoke of those tattoos either, but they spoke volumes of her.

"I did grow up on an island," she said.

"Which island?" Redson asked immediately.

"A hidden island where lost orphans find themselves orphans no more." She picked up the tome on the table between them and flipped it open—Mikal's most recent work. Her gesture seemed to suggest that little nugget of pebble talk was all she wished to say about her origins.

Redson leaned back against the sofa. "Snow," he said, and Angel looked over the book's brim at him. "That cannot really be your last name. *Snow*."

Angel sighed and closed the tome. "I had no last name in my earliest seasons, Redson. So, I took the very dust of Winter as my name. Because it's from the Winter dust that I was made, so that is who I am." She tilted her head, her dark hair slipping over her shoulder. "The snow of Winter was my mother and my father. And I *was* raised by fairies. That is all."

Redson released a long breath. "All right, have it your way. But I'll figure it out in a merry measure. Folk can't keep secrets from someone like me."

Angel's mouth twisted into a smile, assuring him that was *exactly* what she planned to do. But her smile faded, and she clasped her thin fingers. "What else bothers you?" she asked.

Yes, raised by a fairy indeed. Angel's intuition made her unlike most of the Rime Folk Redson knew who hardly noticed when he had a thing or three on his mind.

Redson tapped his thumbs together. "Why do you think Elowin hasn't shown himself to me yet? Am I less important than Cora and Charlie?"

Angel blinked. "By that logic, we're all less important than Cora and Charlie."

"Do you think so?" Redson sat up straighter, and Angel

released an unfeminine grunt whilst rolling her eyes.

"*No*, Redson. I do not think that. And you shouldn't think such a thing either. Elowin will show up at the right time. Stop expecting him to sort out matters on *your* schedule. You need to get yourself on *his*."

Angel's words rang through Redson's mind long into the Winter night.

Mikal

The once-Legionnaire closed his eyes to soak in the warmth of the rising sun over the forest. He listened to the beam of shining light whisper its story through its heat and brilliance. In the trees above, a collection of birds gathered. Mikal peeked an eye open to see them. He was sure they were watching him.

Mikal reached for his shepherd staff, slowly, worried those birds might swoop and peck at him. One of them shuffled on its branch, dislodging a single silver feather. It floated down on the breeze, so Mikal raised a gloved hand to catch it. It glowed rather remarkably when he held it up to the pure sunlight.

"Are you all lost?" he asked the birds.

They blinked at him. A bird or three hopped along the branches to get comfortable. None responded.

Mikal tilted his head in thought. "What is your story, I wonder?"

They all went perfectly quiet at the same time as though they were limbs of one spirit, filling the trees like a congregation awaiting a tale. Mikal had the most unusual urge to start telling them stories.

"Brother." Redson came into the trees with a bothered speck on his brow. "Are you certain of all this?" he asked.

"Of what?" Mikal stole one last suspicious glance at the birds, then tucked the silver feather into his belt and let the creatures be.

"Of our work here. Are you certain we've not turned to mad spinbugs? The Legion is searching for our scotchers, and we've overtossed the remainder of our timestrings for this *mission*. What if we made the wrong choice?"

Mikal did not have to be an Ink Whipper to read the story Redson was telling.

"Brother, don't be afraid to believe," he said, using his shepherd staff as a walking stick as he made his way back out of the forest. Redson followed along, chatting all the while.

"But it's riddlesome, don't you think? We've been at this for a good measure and still this *king* we serve has not turned up—Why are we telling the folk that he has come when he's not even around? His timing is *wrong*, brother. The others can't see it, but I do."

Mikal dragged a hand through his buttery-brown locks. "I suppose you want me to talk to them."

"Well, yes, if you wouldn't mind. We need to make them understand!" Redson huffed.

But Mikal shook his head. "I can't do that."

"Why frostbitten not?"

"I think you and I have been given a task, Redson. The most important task of all." Mikal stopped walking, his fingers sliding around the cane.

"A task…" Redson folded his burly arms and flexed. "What sort of task?"

Mikal took another odd look at the birds in the forest's branches. A small army standing at attention.

"I had a dream yesternight. It unfolded like a story. In it, I saw that in a few seasons' time, Winter grows dark," he said. "Its lights begin to flicker. But you and I prepare for it by going beyond the underground cathedral of the Red Kingdom. We go into the rest of Winter and speak of the good news. We grow two armies; one will carry the Truth into the dark corners, and the other will fight to protect the Truth at all costs. You are a teacher of the sacred truths, and when Elowin comes, he will give your students a tool to always keep the Wisdom with them. And as for me, I raise a generation of guardians to protect that Wisdom, and those Carriers, and to ensure the Truth is never snuffed out."

When Mikal finished, Redson was quieter than he had been in a good measure. He worked his jaw. "But what if we do all that, brother, and Elowin still does not show himself like you hope?"

A bird began to sing in the woods above them. And then another, and then one more.

Soon, the whole congregation hummed at different pitches, a tune so well crafted it made the Migraithe brothers turn to look. The birds ended their praise by holding a powerful note, then lifted from the branches, spiralling into the sky one after the other in perfect order.

"He will," Mikal said as the familiar song of Winter remained, echoing through the trees' bones as though the birds were still singing it. "I think he is already showing himself."

On a dark night when the moon was shielded by navy clouds and even the Winter stars did not breathe light onto the snow's surface, Mikal found himself pacing the halls of Room Four Hundred Plus Six. He paused by the Hall of Doors. Ten plus five doors, all locked until their correct time. Opened only by Cora and her special set of keys. For a reason he could not explain, Mikal felt a soft tug from the Hall, as though one of the doors was trying to tell him something.

But he was too sleepy for a midnight adventure.

He passed the stone kitchen where John Dough was up late baking pastries and filling the space with the warm scents of sugar and bread. The baker was always humming— off tune though. Always humming and always off tune.

Mikal found himself before the fire in the main room. All was quiet and still, except...

Cora shuffled by the patched-up front door as she put on her burgundy cloak. Mikal headed that way, his gaze flickering to where his shepherd staff leaned against the wall by the tea kettle. "You're not really thinking of going to fetch Juniper and Wade alone, are you?"

"Of course I am," was all Cora said as she bent to tighten the laces of her palace slippers. Beside her rested a velvet satchel, open at the top, with lace masks and palace clothes spilling out.

"Do you think that's wise?"

"Do you think I will listen to you even if you try sputtering verses at me, Migraithe?" She stood as she said it, and Mikal blinked.

"Very well, then. Shame on me for forgetting you'd rather eat yellow snow than accept help from one of us." His lashes fluttered as he feigned stifling an eye roll, making sure she saw it. "Shall I get Charlie? Perhaps you'd rather cast insults at him if you're moody, though he will probably agree with me about this," he suggested, nodding toward the hall.

"And I thought Redson was the chatty one," Cora mumbled. But she stood straight and smoothed down her cloak. "I'm not moody. Just…there's a lot at stake. Tonight is *The Golden Mask Eve*. That is why I am going after Juniper and Wade, so I can sneak them out while every folk's identity is concealed. But I cannot look after you if you try to follow me there, Mikal. So please, just let me do this alone as I always do."

"Alone *as you always do*? You have not been alone for many quarters now, Cora. And besides," Mikal crossed the room and picked up the shepherd staff from the wall, "I still have my Ruby Legion uniform. Seems like folly to waste that."

"Redson will be unmerrily ubbersnugged that you left him out of this," she remarked, but she folded her arms to wait. It seemed that was invitation enough, and Mikal smiled as he turned to go find his old uniform.

"I'll be coming too." Charlie appeared from the hall in a red-stitched vest with a claret-ribbon belt. A golden mask covered the top half of his face, and even his fingers were stacked with thin gold and copper rings. Mikal glanced at Cora to see what she would say about it.

Her face was white.

"Oh, have some cheer, Red," Charlie said, crossing the room and reaching past her for the door handle. "I want to see what this Sullen Sprit-Spellborrow looks like." With that, Charlie was out the door and into the Winter night.

"Wait!" Angel came rushing from the hall in a satin floor-length gown of blooming rosettes. A thin fabric mask covered her face also. She brushed by and was out in the cold just as fast as Charlie had been.

Mikal hid his next smile as he hurried to get changed.

The palace was bright with life, the air glittering with luxurious gowns, bronze head wreathes, and poisoned ideology. Mikal slid on his mask and marched through the palace entrance alongside Angel and her date, Charlie, who was otherwise known as Lord Ronnalin on this night. No one questioned the Legionnaire and the well-dressed lord and lady strolling into the palace behind him, along with the other guests crowding in from the Scarlet City.

Some guests had tickets for the ball. Others stopped by the entrance guards to have their names checked off a list. And even others who were familiar to those guarding the doors were waved through without question. But Mikal was a Ruby Legionnaire this eve, and he was not stopped.

Mikal heard Angel giggle and Charlie mumbling jests through a grin. Considering Charlie had been dragged before the Crimson King during his last visit, and had nearly been tossed into the arena, Mikal thought the Green would be a measure more nervous than he was. But there was a certain electricity in the air, and Mikal let it fuel him. He ducked his head as he passed Legionnaires he once knew, and he searched the crowd for Cora who had arrived ahead of time to get dressed for the ball in her room.

The plan was for Cora would go to the dungeons to release Juniper and Wade, then tuck them into a closet so they could dress for the ball. Mikal, Charlie, and Angel would wait for them at the dance floor, and they would all walk out the front door together.

They were *not* planning to open a door to Room Four Hundred Plus Six. If a band of Legionnaires followed them in, it would be a death sentence for all hiding inside.

Mikal noticed Charlie's gaze catch on the cages lining the lobby where Green traitors were imprisoned. Angel studied them, too. But the couple found their smiles as they entered the large ballroom with candle-lit tables of glistening beverages and the sour aroma of plums.

Mikal headed off to the side to stand guard, keeping a good measure away from the other Legionnaires. Charlie and Angel slipped into the crowds to mingle, and after a moment, Charlie tugged Angel into the dancing couples. Mikal watched the girl stifle a laugh.

A tale was being spun from the curtains and chandeliers and from the Rime Folk who sang and danced to the flutes and fiddles. It was different than what Mikal had heard the last time he was in the palace. He had never noticed it before—the murmur ruffling the fabrics when no one was looking and wisping out the flame of a candle like a serpent of wind.

Mikal's thoughts drifted to Cora as he looked over his shoulder, getting the most unusual sensation that he was being watched. He released a silent prayer into the atmosphere so it might charge through the palace and fight on Cora's behalf.

SIXTHLY

Cora

The basement of the Red Kingdom palace was bathed in torchlight, the rumbles of those dancing above echoing deep into the hallway's throat. Cora whisked through the streams of rippling gold, stealing a torch as she came into the dungeons.

"I wish to see a prisoner," she said to the Ruby Legion guards at their posts. "I have permission from the Crimson King himself. I have been sent to—"

"Yes, Lady Thimble." One of the Legionnaires bowed, and Cora's blood warmed.

Lady Thimble.

She glanced down at her costume, her gloved fingers brushing the black mesh veil and velvet-yellow mask concealing her face. She hadn't a clue how the guards recognized her. And now that they had, she was not sure what to do.

"It's your voice, my lady. I recognized it from the Tournaments." The Ruby Legionnaire smiled, proud of himself.

"Ah. Yes." Cora's infamous voice shook.

"Take all the time you need." The Legionnaires stepped aside, one even lifting an arm to welcome her into the moist, mouldy space.

Cora stepped into the dungeon, swallowing a swarm of nerves. As soon as she rounded the corner, she broke into a run on her glass heels as she scanned the cages. But when she saw no faces she recognized, she slowed.

"Juniper!" she finally whispered into the space.

A measure of prisoners shuffled.

"Wade?" she tried again, spinning once.

"Cora?" Juniper's voice lifted from down the line, and Cora sprinted that way. She met Juniper at the bars.

"Cora…" Juniper croaked. "They're going to put us in the arena. They're going to make us fight that young witch who commands the snow!"

"You're not going to face the witch." Cora rifled through her pocket for her ring of keys and drew it out. She pushed the right key into the lock, a loud *click* reverberating down the hall when she turned it.

"Cora…you don't really expect to…" Wade appeared by the door. Dark bags were beneath his eyes. "I mean, how are you planning to get us out?"

Cora shuffled up her skirts and unfastened the rolled satchel from her leg. "There's a closet close by where you can change. I'll distract the Legionnaires so you can pass through the dungeon entrance. Hurry!"

A pinch later, Cora came out of the dungeon with her veil flipped back to show the smile upon her satin-red lips. "Do you mind if I…" Cora did not finish her sentence. Instead, she reached to knock a finger against the hilt of the closest Legionnaire's sword. "I've always wanted to hold one," she said, ensuring her bright gray eyes twinkled.

The Ruby Legionnaire hesitated. "My lady, you're going to get our scotchers into trouble," he said, but he smiled and drew his sword anyway. Cora accepted it with an awed face and swung it through the hall.

Both Legionnaires sprang into action—one going for the sword, the other swerving to catch Cora before the weight of the blade tipped her over. She caught herself against the wall. "I suppose you will have to teach me a thing or three of swordplay, Legionnaires," she said, forcing a laugh.

From the corner of her eye, she watched Juniper and Wade tiptoe past and duck around the bend. Cora handed the sword back. "Another day, though. I have a ball to attend."

She abandoned the Legionnaires and swept down the hall until she caught up with her allies. "Do not stop for anyone. Even if I am stopped, just keep walking to the ballroom. Migraithe and Snow will get you out. And…Charlie is here, too," she whispered to them in the dark.

Two gilded facemasks tilted toward her and nodded.

They took the servants' tunnels. Apart from an attendant or three, no one gave the trio any attention. Cora returned her veil, hoping it would do a better job this time of concealing her identity.

The hinges squeaked when she opened the metal slat-door and ushered her friends from the tunnels. Juniper grabbed her hand as they passed, and Cora was certain she had made the right choice in coming here this eve.

Fiddle songs and laughter trickled from the ballroom. When they entered, it was a hive of golden masks and crimson gowns, sparkling lights, and tipsy dancers. Cora heard Juniper's breath shuddering behind her, and her own knees weakened with nerves.

"Miss Thimble." The voice was dark and rough, and Cora felt the words crawl over her shoulders. She stopped. So did Juniper and Wade.

"Keep walking," she whispered to those at her right and left. Without looking back, her allies disappeared into the golden crowd, leaving Cora to turn and face Sullen Sprit-Spellborrow alone.

Sullen's mask was entirely see-through, barely a mask at all. Just a collection of fiery rust-orange gems placed carefully around his eyes, and a tetrad of silk black feathers poking from his eyelashes.

"Mr. Spellborrow." It was a Winter miracle that Cora's voice did not shake.

He stepped in, taking her gloved hand in his bare one, and ushered her backward into the moving dancers. "I spoke with the Directors about you. It's why you haven't been scolded yet," he said.

Cora's face changed. "I did not ask you to do that." In fact, she had strongly implied she wanted the opposite.

"You don't need to ask me, Cora. If it weren't for me, you would have been made into a disgrace by now. I do not intend to let that happen." Sullen scanned the room with his crisp stare. His eye caught on something, but Cora did not dare look back to see what it was. She swallowed, wishing upon the Winter stars that Juniper, Wade, and her other friends had left.

"You should be thanking me…" But Sullen's brows twitched, and his face pinched together. "Do you hear that?" he asked.

Cora's ears were filled with the pebble talk of the nobles. The flute's sharp racket was nearly painful, and the clinking of glasses never ceased. "I hear all of it," she said.

"No…" Sullen dropped a hand and turned to look about the room. "*That*. Do you hear it?" He rubbed his temples viciously, dislodging one of the black feathers by his eye. Cora watched it float to the floor. "It's like…a whole *symphony* of melodies." Sullen whipped around, tearing his other hand from Cora's. His eyes darted from folk to folk, a wild look upon his face.

Cora tilted her ear to the room. But it was not a bothersome or dreadful sound she heard seeping through the clatter, brushing up her fingers when it reached her. It was a merry tune of glory. A carol.

A mere crack of a smile breached her red-painted lips, but she bit it away. She would scold Charlie for not leaving in a hurry.

"I'm afraid I must go, Sullen. I'll leave you to your…mystery." Cora squeezed Sullen's arm in a dismissal, taking the opportunity to vanish into the moving ocean of masks before Sullen tried to pull her into another dance. She slipped through sash and slipper, crystal bead and speckled light. But when a body moved in front of her, Cora hadn't time to redirect before his hands took her sides and swooped her into a lift in time with the other dancers.

Cora's stomach dropped, but Charlie was smiling. He

brought her down, folding her against his chest and twirling her out for the next step. Her skirts flared with the whine of the fiddles, and when he tugged her back, he finally turned her toward the palace exit.

"Quit messing with Sullen's head, Green," Cora whispered as she grabbed his hand and pulled him toward the lobby.

"I'm merely humming my favourite hymn. It's not my fault if his darkness is recoiling at the sound of it." But Charlie's grip tightened in hers and he suddenly tugged her back. Cora saw why when Legionnaires began filing into the lobby. They blocked the view of whatever was happening by the palace entrance.

"No…" Cora whispered, moving to bolt for the lobby where Wade and Juniper had gone, but Charlie held her tight.

"You'll be revealed if you go, Cora," he said, pushing her back into the crowd and heading for the lobby himself.

Just then, a feminine shout came from the ballroom.

Angel Snow appeared at the edge of the dance floor, dual-bladed sword drawn and glistening in the chandelier light. Cora blanched as the warrior lifted a tanned leg and kicked back the nearest Legionnaire.

Charlie halted where he was.

"Come now, Reds! Play the merry carols!" Angel yelled at the musicians in the corner who had stopped performing amidst the commotion. She tossed her head back and released high, crazed laughter, displaying her throat tattoos. "I welcome your greatest Legionnaires to face me in this ballroom!" She opened her arms wide.

Charlie changed his mind and turned back, taking Cora's hand as Angel whacked away a Ruby Legion spear. "She's causing a distraction," he whispered. "She can only be doing this for one reason—to give Migraithe time to get the others out of the palace. Something must have gone wrong."

"I cannot leave her here to fight them," Cora objected.

"She will catch up to us."

Charlie, who did *not* know the turns of the palace, wove his way around the nobles toward the back doors of the room. "We should not be seen together though," he seemed to realize, "or you'll become a suspect if I'm caught."

Without a discussion, Charlie split away and Cora stopped rushing after him.

She looked back to see Angel kicking her fairy-blessed self off the wall and sailing into the ceiling heights—*impossibly* high. Her black hair whipped as she landed in the middle of the room where guests of the ball screamed and parted.

The silver-marked warrior waited for another Legionnaire to dare challenge her with all these folk racing every which way. She glanced at Cora.

Cora shook the fog from her mind and ran like the rest of the nobles.

Folk pushed her right and left as she moved for the back doors and through the palace halls. Her heels crashed over the tiles, her heart pumping as she slammed every step loudly, blazing a path of sound for the one she knew would follow.

She bounded up the wide staircase to the door of her room, and she flung herself inside, nearly crashing into Charlie who caught her.

"She's coming! Look out!"

Charlie obeyed, yanking the door wide just as Angel barrelled in, skirts and all, and he slammed it shut again. Cora's hands trembled as she drew out her keys.

"If anyone saw…" she rasped. She thrust the copper key into the lock of her own bedroom door and twisted. When she swung it open again, a startled Redson looked back from the other side, standing at the end of the Hall of Doors in his nightwear, a half-eaten ginger cookie in his fingers. Charlie and Angel jumped through, but Cora did not follow. She shot Charlie an apologetic look when he spun back.

"They'll know if I disappear with you." It was the only explanation she gave as she slammed the door shut between them, sealing her allies away and cutting off the path to Room Four Hundred Plus Six.

They could not come back for her.

And she would not risk opening another door to them.

Ruby Legionnaires shouted in the halls, banging on doors and questioning the palace dwellers. Cora walked to her bed and sat, gripping the post with white knuckles and lifting a shaking finger to smear off her lip stain. She sorted through what she would say once they came for her to ask their questions.

SEVENTHLY

Redson

On the sheets of the Pebble Paper, the scribes of the Red Kingdom claimed there were ten plus two "Rime Mice" hiding in the kingdom's shadows, too afraid to come out and face the Crimson Court after all their criminal scheming.

It angered Redson to read such a thing. For none in his company did their work for themselves, but always for others. Always for Elowin—the True King of even the Crimson Court who rejected him. Redson had done a good measure of things in service to Elowin these quarters past.

Yet, Redson did not know what Elowin looked like.

There was a clatter in the Hall of Doors and a flit of low voices. The once-Legionnaire halted his cookie-eating and gaped at the door flinging open at the end of the hall, through which two of his allies hurdled.

Cora slammed the door shut in the same second Charlie sprang for it and tore it back open. But nothing was on the other side of that door now—only a dark cellar with pickled snow prunes. The path had been sealed, and Cora had been sealed away along with it.

Charlie slammed the door shut again. "*Frostbite!*" The jolliest of Elowin's dozen rattled the Winter curse into the air.

"What the windy-wart happened?" Redson dropped his cookie and rushed into the Hall. "Where were you all?!" He looked down at his bland nighty, all too aware of their fine garments.

Angel's face was dismal when she made eye contact. "We rescued Juniper and Wade," she explained.

As though the warrior-who-was-supposedly-raised-by-fairies had summoned it, a loud knock sounded on the front door of Room Four Hundred Plus Six. Redson moved warily for it, pausing to look back at his three friends in the Hall.

He flung the door open, and a bubble of relief filled his chest at the sight of Wade and Juniper shivering and peeling off golden masks outside. Mikal stood with them in a tattered Legion cape—blood trickled from a fresh gash on his elbow.

Redson rushed out to help Juniper stand, tugging the knit housecoat from his shoulders and wrapping her in it. "We're alive," he heard Juniper breathe to Wade with a tear in her eye. "We're home."

Edward appeared by the Hall of Doors, John Dough, Ribble, Jerry, and Bash a step behind—also in their night-clothes. It seemed the Cord of a Dozen Strands was all together again.

Except Cora.

Redson glanced at that closed door. Charlie leaned his back against it, his hair muddled as though he had dragged his fingers through it a thousand times.

Ribble and Jerry brought warm blankets for Wade and Juniper, and John disappeared into the kitchen, likely to bake some sort of ginger-feast. Edward remained—a touch of rust in his gold eyes.

Somewhere in Room Four Hundred Plus Six a door slammed, but not like it was being shut. Rather, it sounded as though someone had flung it open in a hurry and it had collided with the wall. Everyone froze, but a faint glow of shimmering dust puffed around the corner, and after it marched Gathadriel.

"The time has come, Prince," he said to Edward. "We must leave."

"Now?" Edward's eyes sank to an even deeper shade of orange.

"Immediately. The Red Kingdom has flipped over backwards." He held up a slice of ivory parchment with bloodred ink scribbled across it. "They've just announced the reward on your sputtlepun head."

"There is a reward for all of us," Edward objected, nodding toward Angel and Mikal.

"But *you* are my assignment, Edward. And the Ruby Legion is going door to door to hunt for you even as we natter here. It's time to go. Say your goodbyes."

Edward dragged his gaze back to his friends. He settled it on Charlie.

Charlie's chest still heaved, but he cast his friend a modest nod. "This is best. The fairy is right. We will see you again, my King."

"Don't call me that," Edward whispered, a glass film coating his eyes.

"It's what you are," Charlie said through heavy breaths. "Get out of here, Edward. *Our* mission is here—not yours. A day will come when you will be needed, but it's not today." It seemed to pain Charlie Little to say the words, but once they were out, Edward shut his mouth.

The Prince of the Pines nodded slowly. "Until we meet again, friends." He turned away and followed the fairy to the door.

The fairy took one last look at the group. "May the forces of Winter save you in these coming days of darkness." His low voice rippled through the Hall.

A moment later, Gathadriel and the Green prince were gone.

Redson glanced back to where Charlie was slumped against the door, Mikal was gripping the shephards' staff in his Legionnaire uniform, and Angel was eyeing the crumpled Pebble Paper in Redson's fist.

"So Elowin's fairy will protect Edward, but not us?" Redson blurted.

"Don't muddle your buttons over it, brother," Mikal advised, passing by to leave the Hall of Doors.

"Edward is Gathadriel's assignment. The fairy is doing what he is told." Charlie finally lifted off the door and drifted out of the Hall after Mikal.

"*We* are the ones being savagely lied about in the newssheets," Redson said, waving the ball of paper in the air, "yet Elowin has sent no one to protect *us*."

Angel shook her head. "You're filling your mind with garbage, Redson. You'll become mindswept if you keep—"

"Why won't Elowin show himself to me?" Redson cut her off and folded his arms over his chest.

Angel halted. She glanced at Charlie who had paused.

The choir director turned back, skin taught. "I do not know, Redson. I do not know *anything* anymore. I do not know why Elowin chose to show himself to me and not to you," Charlie said. "Nor do I know why he has not shown himself to me again since that first day. But we're going to be spinbugs at dawn if we don't all get some rest, and perhaps some clarity will come with the morning."

"But it doesn't make a pinch of sense!" Redson fought. "I have served this cathedral. I am one of the *dozen*. I am the same as you!"

Angel huffed and walked past him, disappearing into the living space. Redson watched her drag a blanket off the back of the sofa and toss it over her bare shoulders.

"I don't know what to tell you, Redson." Charlie looked defeated.

"Yes. You've *said* that. But am I to continue believing in something I have not seen for myself? Am I to just take your word for it for the remainder of my timestring? How do I even know Elowin exists? How do I know Cora hasn't made this whole thing up just to protect herself because she doesn't want to be a Director of Tournaments?" He cracked the question like a whip, and Charlie's face changed. "It would make sense, wouldn't it? For her to surround herself with strong, gifted people so she could avoid being dragged into the Red Kingdom palace's twisted games."

"Redson!" Mikal snapped.

The air turned heavy with a silent moment's passing.

Charlie's throat bobbed. "In case you haven't noticed,

Redson, of all of us in Room Four Hundred Plus Six, I am the one folk left here who stands out. I am now the only Green in the Red Kingdom. Why would I choose to stay here and fight for a kingdom not my own if Elowin did not exist? Why would I come up with a tall tale to stay here?"

Redson's gaze dropped to the wooden floors. His jaw shifted back and forth. "Why hasn't Elowin shown himself to me?" he asked again.

"Frostbite, Redson! Perhaps he *is* showing himself to you!" There had only been a small measure of times Redson had seen Charlie Little lose his composure.

"If he was showing himself to me, I'd have seen him. I've been looking for the fellow for almost three quarters!"

Charlie's gaze dropped to the Pebble Paper in Redson's fist. "Then you're not looking in the right direction."

When he left, Redson stood perfectly still, listening to the sound of Charlie's footsteps until the door of the Green's room shut behind him.

With a stifled growl, the once-Legionnaire strutted down the hall to his own space, barging in and slamming the door with a ruckus. "Why not me, Elowin?" he muttered into the dark. "Why them and not me?"

It wasn't a real prayer, as far as he was concerned, but Redson stilled as he sensed the whisper grow wings and lift off in flight. Feeling a strange tightening on his skin, he sank down onto his bedspread and decided to be quiet after that.

EIGHTHLY

Sullen Sprit-Spellborrow

The palace buzzed like a hive of blue wasps, but the racket hardly touched Sullen's occupied mind.

The authorities of the Crimson Court spilled into the meeting room behind him as he stared out the long crystal window at the Scarlet City. Falling snow mixed with heavy mist, blanketing the white stone buildings and lanterns lining the onyx streets. Tiny specks of light escaped the fog that choked out all the other colours.

Court members barked at each other, shaking their drinks and pointing their fingers as they tried to decide who was to blame for the mishap at *The Golden Mask Eve*, and how that treacherous blue-haired sputtlepun had gotten into the palace past the Ruby Legionnaires standing guard. But, most especially, they argued about how she had gotten *out* of the palace again after the scene she had made.

Sullen peeled the gold stones off the flesh around his eyes. His golden mask had not held up through the evening. The scribe's bright eyes took in the view of the city's twisted streets and bent steeples, yet over and over again he saw *that* face and heard *that* voice.

A youthful Rime man had been on Cora Thimble's arm at the ball. The folk had a modest pair of eyes and an easy smile…but his voice was pure chaos. Sullen's inner spirits had shuddered when the tune had reached his ears. But the worst part was, for a reason Sullen could not weave together, Cora had seemed affectionate toward the musical being.

If only the folk had not been wearing a mask. Sullen might have followed him. He might have questioned him.

He might have killed him.

"What do you mean the she-folk *disappeared?*" The Crimson King's voice cracked through the room. "One does not just disappear into the air."

"We chased her down the hall, but when we reached the top of the stairs she'd vanished. We checked every door, every room. But she's no longer in this palace," a Legionnaire promised in a trembling voice.

"I'm certain she is in league with the Green prince. How do these enemy criminals keep slipping away from my Legionnaires?" The king's ring-adorned fist slammed a table. "It's not as though they can hop through windows encased with ancient Winter magic! We must be able to trap them somehow!"

"Yes, yes. We keep the windows locked anyway. Only the head palace steward has the key." The mediator waved a hand and slipped a pair of gold spectacles onto his face as he lifted a page of notes.

More discussion broke out, but Sullen's yellow gaze lifted slowly.

With the glorious lamplights at his back, he could see his reflection in the window. He imagined leaping through the crystal and ending up somewhere else entirely. Ending up in the reflection, trapped inside the glass for the remainder of his timestring.

Winter's magic could be a tricky thing. But Sullen had the inkling this was something else as he pictured that young musical folk from the ball again and remembered how Cora's hand had swept over the sputtlepun's wrist as he guided her along. Where had they been going? They had both disappeared after the ball. Just like the blue-haired shefolk.

Sullen's jaw tightened as a familiar clanking of metal filled his mind. He always knew Cora was near when he heard that sound. He dreamt of that sound, following it through the dark channels of his mind until he found her in his sleep. Cora Thimble—always with a large ring of rattling keys.

A growl escaped him, and Sullen raised a hand to flick his reflection.

Of course folk were always disappearing, always *escaping*. Cora Thimble had a set of magic keys.

Sullen shook his head in disbelief, prepared to scream at himself for never noticing. She was too pretty—that was the problem. He had never questioned Cora's absences at the palace, the odd way she came in through the side doors, her lack of desire to impress the Directors of Tournaments.

It was her.

Her.

It was Cora Thimble. She had been stringing Sullen along, making a fool out of him.

Though he wished to shout it from the palace roof, Sullen did not reveal his revelation to those in his company. Rather, he tilted his head and closed his eyes, calling out through the darkness.

It's Cora Thimble, his mind whispered to the one he was truly pledged to. The presence. The simmering, deep beastly thing that had guided him thus far. *She's the liar in our midst.*

A hungry, bone-chilling growl rippled through Sullen's mind in response; a sound that seeped up from below the Red Kingdom that none in the room at his back would hear.

If only Sullen had seen Cora for what she was. He might have dragged her into her own arena and left her to the mercy of the Directors she was meant to impress.

A voice lifted from the snow. With it came the low screams of ice-crows and the cries of tormented souls in fury.

Kill the Master of Keys, Cora Thimble. Deliver to me her ashes of snow.

The instruction punched through Sullen's chest, and he inhaled, bracing a flat hand against the window to steady himself. His chest rose and fell as he felt the presence of others tuning in to the command also. Listening ears across the kingdom picked up the sound of their master. The young witch downstairs who ruled the arena, for instance. Or key members of the Crimson Court who had avoided this emergency meeting.

When Sullen's eyes flashed open, the loud natter behind

him flooded back in, the red carpet became steady below his feet, and the city before him came back into focus. His eyes snapped to the left when something moved.

There, sitting on a velvet stool, sat a tiny Red Prince with a silver coronet resting in his mahogany hair. He watched Sullen with curious burgundy eyes. It seemed the boy had snuck away from the meeting. Sullen blinked.

The little prince stuck out his tongue.

Sullen stared at the child as the boy kicked off his palace slippers and began counting his toes aloud in high-toned, barely decipherable words.

Sullen hid his glare and rolled his eyes. A moment later, he pushed away from the crystal window and left the meeting where the Crimson Court argued.

NINTHLY

Cora

The Crimson King called a meeting with the Crimson Court in the middle of the morning. Breakfast had not yet been served and Cora heard her stomach sing a noise of rebellion as she sloshed down the hall in her glittering tule skirts. Pink sunlight streaked the white tiles, filtering in through the stained glass with promises that the snowstorms and cold rains were taking a sabbatical. The light warmed her face, and she stole a glance of the skies beyond the walls that owned her.

Syrup, maple, and melted butter cast their aromas through the halls as Cora rounded the final bend and headed toward the meeting room. She noticed there were no guards outside the large doors. She paused before trying to drag the heavy things open herself when she realized there were no guards *anywhere*.

Cora did a full turn outside the meeting room. She could hear the soft murmurs of nobles inside; she could smell the truthspire's honey-like aroma saturating the air.

Cora sighed and tugged on the doors to make her way in.

The staircase down the middle of the auditorium was mostly clear, but the theatre seats were full. Members of the Crimson Court whispered, giggled, and muttered as they ate candy-covered white apples and sipped truthspire from metal goblets. Cora made it halfway down the stairs before she got the sense that someone was watching her.

Her fingers brushed the rail for balance when she paused, and her skin tightened as she locked gazes with Lord Chestnire across the room. Chestnire's gaze was penetrating, accusatory even. Cora's sights snapped to another head turning in her direction. Lady Shotney fixed her gaze on Cora, too.

Warmth pooled in her belly as she turned to slowly head back up the stairs, suddenly aware of just how many people filled this room. People she had lied to. People she had fooled to keep her underground cathedral safe. People who would want her blood if they discovered her truths.

The rest of the Crimson Court members were snowseas-deep in their pebble talk, not paying her any attention.

She looked back at Lord Chestnire once more, realizing his eyes were darker than the last time she had seen them. She was sure he used to have purple eyes, like the king.

Cora trotted the rest of the way back to the doors and pushed through with a ruckus. She rushed down the hall, blinking against the pink morning light. Her hand brushed her pocket.

The hallway filled with the sound of swords being drawn, and Cora tore the ring of keys from her dress. She fumbled for a key, approaching the first door she saw. She aimed for the lock but faltered with her hand a pinch away, key suspended.

A lock she did not recognize was fitted over the door. Cora tried to press the key in, but it did not fit. She took a step back and looked around for another door.

Her stomach turned. This same lock had been fitted over *every* door. She had not noticed on her walk to the meeting room.

Cora sprang toward her bedroom—the only room with a door she knew had not been changed. She took note of the replaced locks as she passed them.

Twenty plus two new locks. Twenty plus two unusable doors. The entire path between her room and the meeting room had been bound with locks her keys could not fit into.

Cora swept into her room in a tangle of tule, loose hair, and panting. She slammed the door shut, pressing a hand against the swarming colours in her chest and her thudding heart. With the other hand she pulled her keys from her pocket.

A noise sounded behind her, and she jumped, sending the keys slipping from her fingers and clattering to the floor.

Sullen's palace boots shifted slowly as he stepped in perfect silence toward the keys. He studied them for a pinch before reaching down to pick them up, and Cora felt the flush drain from her face. His yellow eyes examined the ring, the keys, the metal teeth. Then they flicked up to Cora.

Cora took one last look at her keys in his delicate fingers. And then she swung open the door, and she ran. Sullen's growl echoed down the hall after her.

She looked from door to door, hall to hall, stair to stair. She picked a staircase and tapped her way down, the thudding of Sullen's palace shoes only a breath behind.

She darted around a bend, slipped into a servants' tunnel, and slammed the door shut. In distant hallways, orders were being shouted. Palace boots thudded over tiles.

Cora followed the tunnel to the ballroom. The door clattered as she burst out and crossed the open floor. In the same heartbeat, she slid into another servants' tunnel, nearly stumbling over a dislodged stone in the darkness.

When she made it to the basement's laundry caves, she came out and flashed a convincing smile at the palace attendants scrubbing uniforms, and she fled through the back entrance into the attendants' villa.

Cora had never lived anywhere except at the palace. She had never known another life apart from Red traditions, lush gowns, trays of sweets, and twisted games.

She had not even had time to bring her cloak.

Cora spent the first eve away from the Red palace in the shadow of the tea houses, dreaming of a warm cup of herbal remedies in her hands. Dreaming of the special brews Mikal always had percolating in the lobby of Room Four Hundred Plus Six. She thought of John Dough's ginger snaps and the warm fireplace where Angel frequently basked to ease her chill. And Charlie...

She thought of his smile which had always been able to warm any room.

When shuffles sounded behind her at midnight, Cora led the Legionnaires through a series of twists and turns around the city until she swept into the courtyard of a noble's chateau and ducked into an empty barrel out back. Tears squeezed out the corners of her eyes as she tried to warm her cold fingers. They had gone numb at the nails.

When the Legionnaires gave up trying to find her, she slipped back into the city's heart.

Sleigh bells rang through the nighttime air, and Cora huddled against a stone wall, clutching her arms to herself with chattering teeth as the stars appeared, passed over the Winter skies, and disappeared once again to make way for the glow of early morning.

The second eve she spent in the city was less cold, but frightfully damp. It seemed the brief sunlight from yester-morning had held false promises, and the icy rain came down in sheets. Cora's hair stuck to her neck, the water blurring her vision as it rolled down her forehead and smothered her eyes. She trudged by elves in long coats hoisting up satin umbrellas, and a time or three she saw hooded figures watching her from the shadows.

She laughed in despair when she realized she had not escaped at all.

Her heart toiled with its choices—to go back to Room Four Hundred Plus Six and risk leading Sullen's spies to the entrance of her cathedral, or to leave the Red Kingdom and not look back.

In the morning, Cora awoke to the sound of birds. She blinked at the hazy sun trying to break through the city's mist. She brought a hand up to rub her eyes and began peeling away the layers of apple-sacks she had hidden beneath.

Her legs wobbled as she tried to stand. She had not eaten anything but a few half-rotted slices of apple from the pie factory's disposal crates. She was so very tired. So very hungry. But none of that mattered.

Last night she has resolved a thing or three. She had to get out of the Red Kingdom before she was found, or the Crimson Court would use terrible force to get her to reveal where the believers were hiding.

"Move it! I can't help a peg out of its shell like you." An elf in an embellished apron came from the back door of the factory waving a hand through the air. "Leave or I'll shout for the Legion!" he threatened, and Cora nearly stumbled at the mention.

She straightened herself—her tule skirts, her hair—and she marched off.

"Wait a pinch…" the elf called after her, bringing Cora to stop. He drew a newssheet from his pocket and studied it, then he looked back at Cora. "Is this you?" The elf turned the Pebble Paper around, and Cora's mouth turned dry.

There in the column was a drawing of Cora's face, with sharp gray eyes and a touch of rosy in her cheeks.

"No," she lied, turning and shuffling away.

But the elf was not convinced. "Legionnaires! *Legionnaires*!" he cried.

Cora broke into a sprint toward the black roads. She rounded two bends, slipped through an alley, ducked beneath a bridge, and raced up the roadside, searching for an unwatched reindeer she might borrow. She screamed when her hand struck a brick wall she had been trying to sidestep, bending her fingers out of shape. She had felt her Rime bone snap in her pinky. The searing pain made her disoriented, and she slowed to a walk as she realized she had become separated from the rest of the crowd.

She did a full turn. She stood in the very centre of the public square, alone. Stationed around the perimeter of the wide, cobbled plaza were Ruby Legion guards with their swords drawn. They looked at her.

Cora's colours dimmed. Her heart sank.

So, this was it then.

TENTHLY

Redson

Though his face was hidden by a navy hood, Redson thought to charge into the public square where Cora stood alone. He watched her shoulders relax, and she stood straight as though accepting her fate. As though she had decided she would allow the ten plus eight Legionnaires surrounding the square to apprehend her; possibly even turn her back into snow right there in the city's centre.

The Migraithe brothers had followed Cora since they heard a folk calling for the Legionnaires behind the pie factory. Cora had come out from the alley so fast, Redson had not been able to call her name.

The brothers had searched for her the whole night prior, along with Charlie, Angel, and Jerry. They'd set out the moment the Crimson Court had disowned their Director of

Tournaments in their Pebble Paper. Sullen Sprit-Spellborrow had called her a *'Rival of the Reds.'*

And now here she was—surrounded and facing death. Redson inched a step closer, nudging aside a folk in a polar bear-skin coat.

"Wait, brother," Mikal's quiet voice slipped over to him.

Redson's fingers tightened around his shepherd staff, but Mikal grabbed his wrist and kept him still, even as the Legionnaires moved in with their swords drawn and their silver spears pointed.

"Cora has fought the good fight," Mikal said. "But we cannot reveal ourselves. We've been given an assignment."

In this moment, Redson could hardly remember the dream Mikal had told him about. He watched Cora's sharp gray eyes slide around the square. She did not even know her friends were close by. She did not realize she wasn't alone. Redson wanted to wave, at least. To catch her attention so she would see them there with her.

Something warm brushed Redson's arm, sending a flit of life into his chest. He glanced over to see who had touched him, and the stirring of his insides came to a halt.

Looking back at him was a pair of eyes as bright as the rising sun with the purples of the stars, the greens of juniper bushes, and the wild topaz of deep snowseas treasure. It was as though the sparks of colour in Redson's chest recognized the colours in this youthful folk's eyes. Mirrored them even. Redson could not breathe. He could not think. The folk looked right at him.

"How about a trade?" the folk offered, reaching out and unfolding his fingers to reveal a plain glass ball.

Redson stood in perfect stillness as the folk reached for

the shepherd staff in his hand. A current of gold script brushed along the folk's wrists. The columns of text went in and out—showing and then disappearing—as he handed Redson the orb.

The folk carried Redson's staff into the square where Legionnaires took Cora roughly by the shoulders.

"It's…" Redson could not utter the name, but he knew who this was. His Rime colours recognized their True King. Redson's mouth hung open as Elowin entered the square.

Cora was pushed to her knees. She closed her eyes as the Legionnaires pulled out wire to bind her wrists. But the guards paused when Elowin arrived.

"Get up," he said in a kind, commanding voice, and Cora's eyes opened. They grew wide, telling Redson that she recognized this folk too. It seemed a Legionnaire or three also recognized him as they dropped their wires and Cora's hands.

Cora rose to her feet. At the very centre of the public square, before the whole Red Kingdom, Elowin reached for her hand and lifted it.

Redson's jaw tightened when he saw her bent fingers— swollen and red all the way to her knuckles. Elowin clasped her trembling fingers in his, and Cora blinked.

When he released her, quiet gasps flitted around the square.

Cora raised her hand. Her fingers were straight, the swelling gone. She waved them through the air, tightened a fist, then stretched them.

"How did he just…"

"Was that a new magic we haven't seen?"

"Is this a trick?"

Redson looked down at the glass orb in his grip as voices lifted from the crowd. A mist seemed to have grown in the orb's middle; it danced as though performing to a song—a song Redson could almost hear. A song for Winter's most silent nights when all was calm and all was bright.

A lady folk sprang from the crowd with a child in her arms. The Ruby Legionnaires shifted, but they did not stop her as she approached Elowin and Cora. "Please!" the woman begged, holding out her child to Elowin. "My beloved child's leg has a bruise. It's brought bad tidings upon our dwelling. Will you heal him?"

Elowin studied the woman and the child. "Thank you for not being too afraid to believe. Your belief has made him well."

Folk moved in, watching in awe as the child's bruise disappeared. But it wasn't just the boy, Rime Folk all over the public square began gasping and crying out in joy as they waved once-broken limbs and found their cuts and scrapes were no more.

A Ruby Legionnaire dropped his spear to the ground. He stared at his own unblemished wrist and fell to his knees in awe.

An aged man with spirally white hair drifted toward Elowin holding a drum. "My drum recognizes you. It has met you before, on the eve of your birth, I'm certain of it," he said, drawing a smile from Elowin. The aged man held out the drum. "It is yours."

But a shrill growl tore over the square, freezing the blood in Redson's body. At his side, Mikal redirected his shepherd staff, holding it out before him as he moved into the square. Redson followed as a folk scrambled away.

Screams erupted from a cloaked sputtlepun. She tore down her hood, revealing the young face that Redson knew from her performances in the arena. He halted his footsteps at the sight of her graying skin and molten black eyes.

"I shall destroy you and your beloveds in the end, Son of the White Kingdom!" The voice that came from the young witch was that of a beast. She roared, sending a spray of black flies into the air, but they dissolved before they reached Elowin. The witch's eyes flickered between pure black and pale, watery blue with a slice of fear. Her head twitched like it was not properly attached.

She spun on her heel and scrambled off.

Redson had not seen a thing so unusual in a measure of seasons. He stared at where the witch had just been.

"Son of the White Kingdom..." someone gossiped from the crowd. "Isn't that a name from the ancient writings?"

Ruby Legion boots thudded over onyx roads nearby, echoing over the city. A hundred plus a hundred more Legionnaires headed their way, led by the purple-eyed Crimson King himself.

Rime Folk in the square began to shuffle off, but the mother of the child remained, reaching into the basket on her arm. "I have a gift for you, in the spirit of the Red Holiday," she said, digging through the basket quickly whilst eyeing the approaching guards in crimson capes. She drew a stick-wreath from her basket. "It's not a true crown, and it's not fit for a king. I only meant to hang it in my window for the Holiday. But it's the only gift I have." The woman swallowed, looking at Elowin a moment more. "I believe you are that folk who was meant to come for us," she whispered.

The woman hoisted her child high on her hip and turned

to flee from the square. The Ruby Legionnaires who had witnessed the full event stood tall and began brushing themselves off at the arrival of the Crimson King, repositioning their weapons. But some cast Elowin unsteady looks.

One Legionnaire Redson recognized sheathed his sword and approached the True King, pulling a large, four-pointed iron star from his chest that marked him as one of the elite among his comrades. He held the star out to Elowin, the shallow cup in the star's centre reflecting the morning light. "Please. Take it. It's my most valuable possession, but I will trade it for the healing of my beloved daughter who now lays in bed waiting to die from the frostbug disease."

When Elowin did not take the star, the Legionnaire fastened it to Elowin's chest, pinning it to his cloak. "Please," the Legionnaire said a time again.

The army marched down the slope toward the public square, dressed in copper and gold as though ready for war.

"She is already healed because of your belief. Go home now and see." Elowin's voice was like the music of the snow, the songs of the birds, and the hum of the Winter forests. It reminded Redson of Charlie's singing.

The Legionnaire nodded quickly. "I shall."

"Get back to your post, Legionnaire!" one of the guards behind him called. Their spears were poised once again; aimed at Elowin. But the guards did not move in to strike, and Redson guessed they were a pinch afraid to try after all they had witnessed.

The Legionnaire stepped back into line with his fellow soldiers and drew his sword, but he did not look prepared to use it.

Elowin turned, his hands filled with a drum and a thorny

wreath, his chest pinned with an iron star. He walked through those of the crowd who were left. Even the Greed parted for him, watching with peculiar stares, shifting back uneasily. Cora, Redson, and Mikal followed him.

LASTLY, AND SO FORTH

In Room Four Hundred Plus Six, Elowin took the drum and rested the thorned wreath atop it. The two fit together in perfect harmony as though the drum itself welcomed the crown's alliance. Inside the wreath, Elowin placed the four-pointed star. He took Redson's glass orb and laid it in the star's shallow cup, and the Cord of a Dozen Strands watched in awe as the drum, the wreath, and the star came to life. Burning ribbons of crimson, scarlet, and gold breathed into the quaint space along with a tune. Gold and cream sparks lit up inside the glass orb, dancing and twirling.

Elowin took Mikal's shepherd staff next. The moment the weapon touched Elowin's fingers, words carved themselves into the staff's surface and thorns of crystal ice sprouted from the staff's hook, creating a masterful, artful weapon of defense.

And on one fine, new, and glorious morn', when Redson and Mikal were preparing to go out into all of Winter to preach the merry news with the tools they had been given, Elowin said to them, "Brothers, you have the most important assignment of all." Redson seemed startled by that, but Elowin went on, "You shall build my army in the seasons to come. It will not be easy. Know that trouble will find you, but fear not! For the end is coming, and I have overcome the Winter world."

FIVE FULL WINTER SEASONS LATER

A

BLAST

OF

SYMPHONIES

The Final Novella

THE PEBBLE PAPER

ON THIS MORN' WE ANNOUNCE A MERRY RE-
WARD PAYABLE TO THE CITIZEN WHO BRINGS
FORTH INFORMATION THAT RESULTS IN THE
CAPTURE OF THE TEN PLUS TWO WHO CALL
THEMSELVES, *THE CORD OF A DOZEN STRANDS*.
THE REWARD WILL CONSIST OF A GIFT OF FOUR
HUNDRED PLUS FIFTY GOLD RINGS AND A PER-
MANENT, FULL-TIME POSITION IN THE ESTEEMED
CRIMSON COURT.

AS ALWAYS, BE CAUTIOUS OF THE IDEOLOGIES
OF THESE FOLLOWERS OF THE ONE CALLED
ELOWIN. THEIR BELIEFS AND PROPHETIC NATTER
WERE DEEMED UNFIT FOR RED SOCIETY MANY
SEASONS PAST AND ARE OFFENSIVE TO US FOLK
OF THE CURRENT TIMES.

AS POSTED ABOVE, IF ANY FOLK CAN BRING
FORTH INFORMATION THAT LEADS TO FINDING
AND SILENCING THE DOZEN, THEY ARE ELIGIBLE
TO ACCEPT THIS REWARD.

IF ANYONE CAN DELIVER THEM TO THE DIREC-
TORS OF TOURNAMENTS, AN EVEN GREATER RE-
WARD SHALL BE PROVIDED.

STAY SAFE. STAY UNITED.
YOUR EDITOR-IN-CHIEF,

Sullen Sprit-Spellborrow

FIRSTLY

Mikal

Season's greetings, Mikal and Redson,

I hope this unmerry message finds you. I trusted it with the birds who promised to carry it across the snows and deliver it to your hand.
I'm heartwrenched to tell you that Jerry and Ribble were captured by the Ruby Legion and handed over to the Directors of Tournaments this eve past. They were brought into the arena and turned back into snow by that sputtlepun witch who calls herself Mara Rouge. I'm grateful they are together in the White Kingdom now.

Though Elowin has been walking the streets of the modest villages on the kingdom's brim these five seasons past—

healing their diseased, stirring their courage, and bringing new believers into the fold—there is such a measure of resistance from the Red Kingdom's prophets and authorities that it's making folk afraid to associate with us.

But many who listen to Elowin believe. All who are ill are healed by him. I have never witnessed a thing like it in all my seasons. Despite the Red Kingdom's resistance, Elowin is changing Winter.

—Cora

Mikal crumpled the note in his palm.

Jerry and Ribble had been good and faithful friends. Mikal was sure he would not be able to eat anything for a measure, lest his stomach force it back up.

Redson would be heartwrenched.

Perhaps it was time to return to the Red Kingdom and reunite with the Cord of a Dozen Strands once again. The only consolation to this dreadful news was that Elowin was taking back the villages in the name of hope. The True King was at work. And even though the skies billowed with gray clouds and whispered dark stories, there was a thing or three bringing cheer to Winter.

The once-Legionnaire trudged through the snow in his silk-laced boots, tugging his black jacket tighter. He tapped his shepherd staff against the snowdrift and the sea of snow parted, making a dry path for him to walk through. He gazed up at the tall cliff of Wentchester Cove, ignoring the bickering natter of the ten plus eight sputtlepuns trailing behind him.

A snowball hit the back of Mikal's shoulder, bringing an eruption of young snorts and giggles, and he stopped walking.

Sputtlepuns.

He sighed.

"Try that a time again, and you'll spend the eve clearing every snowflake from this ice rink *without* your staffs," he warned without turning around.

All the young folk behind him went quiet.

It was a pleasantly peaceful walk through the tunnel after that. Mikal brushed aside the Key Room curtain and found Redson pacing around the large golden sphere that spun slowly and lit the room. Redson held up his own Revelation Orb and the light shone through it, casting columns of words onto the wall. Some of the orb-carrying students had scribbled their names there with ink.

On and on Redson went, talking of old myths and the sacred truths written in the Volumes of Wisdom. Volumes which had been tucked away into hidden libraries around Winter for safe keeping by Mikal himself and a band of merry dwarves he had crossed on his journeys that seemed eager to help.

Mikal used one of those invisible libraries to train the ever-growing group of wild sputtlepuns into guardians. Four hundred plus ten of them had stayed back with the dwarves for this trip. He had selected only a few to accompany him to Wentchester Cove to meet with his brother.

Redson hushed his pebble talk when Mikal entered with the ten plus eight young ones in black. A measure of the boys waved to those in the room they recognized from the times Mikal's sputtlepuns and Redson's sputtlepuns had trained side-by-side.

"Ah. We have company." Redson slapped shut a book, sending a puff of dust into the air.

"I need to speak with you, brother. Alone." Mikal's tone made Redson's face change.

A moment later, the Migraithe brothers were back in the tunnel, leaving the young ones behind. Barely a second had passed before hoots and hollers drifted from the room.

Mikal handed Redson the letter from Cora.

"I think it's time we went back to the Red Kingdom to see our friends," he said.

Redson looked up from the note, his brows bunching together. "I will destroy those Legionnaires," he swore.

"You'll do no such thing. We're needed here, now more than ever. But we'll go aid our friends in their fight until things have settled. Then we'll return to our duties," Mikal said, dipping his shepherd staff toward the Key Room. "Choose a small measure of your Carrier folk to accompany us. My guardian sputtlepuns will protect them. We'll assign them into pairs before we go through the iron gate, and we'll stay together."

"Why bring the sputtlepuns?" Redson asked, handing the dreadful letter back.

Mikal tucked the letter back into his jacket pocket. "Elowin directed us to build this army for him. I want to show him what we've done."

It took three days in a raging snowstorm for the Migraithe brothers to reach the Red Kingdom. The storm provided a welcome cover as they passed through the iron gate, the sputtlepuns huddling together to keep warm.

They met their allies above a cider tavern in a room Redson purchased with a gold ring. And when Angel Snow arrived first, Mikal watched Redson's solemn face melt into a wide, sheepish smile.

"You look as lovely as ever," Redson said, and Mikal stifled the rolling of his eyes.

Angel cast Redson a sweet look which Mikal pretended not to see, and some of the sputtlepun boys snickered.

"Quiet," Mikal reminded them gently. "No one is to know we're here."

Five hooded figures came in next—one of them humming. Mikal felt his shoulders relax at the softness of Charlie's tenor.

"Send the sputtlepuns into the next room so we can speak with our friends," Mikal suggested. Redson nodded and ushered the youth out into the room across the hall.

Cora's mouth parted when she pulled her hood down and took in the modest flock pushing each other through the doorway. "How did you come by so many?" she asked while observing the black clothes of Mikal's guardians, spun from the dwarves' magic threads back in the library. Pure black. Not a stain to be seen. Cora's gaze swept over to Redson's students in white, covered in the same clean threads.

"So many?" Redson huffed a laugh as he sealed the door shut and returned. "This is a small measure of our numbers. There are hundreds more."

"Hundreds?!" Cora's sharp gray eyes widened.

"By the sharpest wind…" Charlie breathed. "In only five seasons?!"

But when the singer lifted his gaze, it flickered. In Charlie's eyes, Mikal saw a story of sorrow clinging to his spirit. He saw the loss of Jerry and Ribble.

Redson had seen it, too. "I wish I could fight them," he said. "One last time, I wish I could stand against the Ruby Legion that has brought so much destruction."

"The folk who lives by the blade dies by the blade, brother," Mikal said, quoting a Volume passage.

"You speak a sacred truth, Mikal Migraithe." A warm voice filled the room, and through the doorway came someone with no hood and not a speck of fear upon his brow. Mikal felt the rest of the words vanish from his tongue. The folk was spun in gold dust with colours like rainbows in his eyes.

The Migraithe brothers stood in silence before their True King.

"We should kneel," Redson whispered to Mikal, seeming unsure if it was a ridiculous notion or not.

"No one else is," Mikal whispered back, though his knee twitched as he thought about it.

"I came to bring good tidings," Elowin told the group. "For things will grow darker still, but you must trust in the light that will come."

It was odd, but Mikal thought the words sounded like a farewell of sorts.

And as it turned out, it was a farewell.

Elowin surrendered himself to the Crimson King the next morning.

SECONDLY

Cora

They took the long way around the Scarlet City to reach the Yard of Ice Stones. Upon pillars of solid ice, folk scribed the names of fallen beloveds. It was here ceremonies were held to remember those who had been turned back into snow, like Jerry and Ribble. There was work to do still—a thing or three waiting back in Room Four Hundred Plus Six—but Cora could not move on until she had paid her friends of many seasons a proper moment of respect.

"He really gave no reason?" John Dough asked with a troubled face. He smelled of icing sugar and sweet cinnamon pastries.

"None at all." Cora stared across the forest of ice pillars, not really seeing it. "Of all the endings Elowin whispered about, this was not the one I anticipated. We're lost without him, John."

John did not object, nor did Angel, Juniper, Wade, or

any of the others listening. The True King of Winter belonged on the highest throne, not in a cold Red Kingdom prison cell, treated as a criminal, spat upon, tormented, and ridiculed by the Crimson Court. It was the worst fate for a folk, and an even worse one for Elowin whom the Reds had openly rejected.

The Migraithe brothers insisted their sputtlepuns should sleep at the tavern during their visit. Redson claimed it was not safe to tell the chatty young folk about Room Four Hundred Plus Six, but Cora did not agree. She had looked upon those youths and seen something remarkable. Their young hearts were the ones most precious in her sight, the ones worth the most in all of Winter. The ones who might push back in the days to come, after the Cord of a Dozen Strands was long gone.

These were Cora's thoughts as she watched Mikal and Redson lead their modest group of sputtlepuns to the Yard of Ice Stones. Her gaze drifted back to the closest stone where Jerry and Ribble's names belonged. She imagined that young witch conjuring the snow with her restless evil in the arena. She imagined the girl turning Jerry and Ribble to snow before a crowd of spectators, the same spectators Cora had been tasked to entertain only five seasons ago. John placed an arm around Cora's shoulders when she shivered.

The ice pillars glistened in the late morning light like a small city of cerulean glass.

"He must have had his reasons," Charlie said after eavesdropping for a while. "Elowin wouldn't surrender himself to the Crimson Court without a reason."

"We'll deal with it after the ceremony," Cora said, but

she felt the same question weighing upon her thoughts, leaking into her logic, crippling her wisdom. She could not figure out why Elowin had abandoned them at a time like this. Why would he allow the Reds to do such cruel things to him? Why, when so much was at stake?

The Migraithe brothers' merry band fanned out, surrounding the yard as Cora stepped forward with Mikal's pocket pen in her fingers. She placed her palm against the ice, feeling the deep pinch of cold. She wanted to feel every speck of pain it brought in this moment, for she had felt rather numb since morning.

She carved her friends' names into the pillar alongside other fallen Rime Folk. She did it knowing she could get arrested for adding the Crimson Court's enemies to the Court-owned yard, but Cora and those in her company were wanted folk anyway.

And Jerry and Ribble had been dear comrades.

Charlie sang a quiet song as Redson stepped forward to natter a speech about Jerry and Ribble. But he stopped mid-sentence when a pair arrived, plummeting from the sky like a falling stone.

Gathadriel's heels slammed into the snow. He dropped Edward Haid at the yard's edge, and the once-prince scrambled to find his footing. Cora felt a rush at the sight of the Green prince whom she had not seen in nearly five full seasons, but it seemed he had stayed alive and well in that time. Charlie made it to Edward first, tugging him into a hug and flashing a smile which Edward returned. Gathadriel stayed back, but he winked at one of Mikal's youngest sputtlepun guardians in raven-black. The boy's eyes widened like he had never seen a fairy before.

The ceremony was short and simple. It was an excuse for those left in the Cord to come together again. Perhaps an opportunity to discuss what Elowin had done and what it might mean for the cathedral moving forward.

But Cora was not certain she could move forward.

Mikal and Redson began leading the sputtlepuns away from the yard just as a series of loud commands lifted past the buildings. Metallic sounds of drawing weapons made a chorus of noise, and Cora's eyes fired to Charlie and Edward.

"Get Edward away from here!" Cora called to Gathadriel. But Gathadriel looked to the young ones in their midst with hesitation, for fairies were known to care the most about children. "Focus on your assignment!" she reminded him with a nod to Edward as the shouts drew closer.

"No, Cora..." Edward's gold eyes shone, but Gathadriel obeyed and scooped up the Green prince. In a pinch, Edward and Gathadriel were lost to the skies, vanishing just as quickly as they had appeared.

Ruby Legionnaires marched around a stone building, red capes fluttering, silver spears pointed at Charlie.

"They were waiting for us here," Juniper whispered, taking a step back. "This was a trap."

Redson shoved his sputtlepuns toward a slim alley with one hand and punched a Ruby Legionnaire with the other. He stole the folk's sword in the process.

"Don't fight them, Redson! Just run!" Mikal yelled as he rushed his own sputtlepuns into the same alley and stood guard at the mouth until the boys were out of sight.

Charlie appeared at Cora's side and Cora was swept away, her fingers interlocked with Charlie's. She glanced back to see Angel drawing her dual-bladed sword to defend Juniper and Wade who were trapped in the yard, and Cora wavered, drawing Charlie to slow down.

Mikal's shepherd staff collided with a Ruby Legion blade as he blocked the Legionnaires from following the sputtlepuns down the alley. Cora's eyes widened as a ribbon of snow burst up from the ground as though Mikal was *telling* it to. It slapped across a Legionnaire's eyes.

But a great roar reverberated down the street, and every folk—Legionnaire and Cord—stilled as heavy footfalls shook the earth. "It sounds like Edward and Gathadriel sent help," Charlie whispered.

Mikal pushed into the crowd of soldiers toward Redson as a tall, white not-snowsquatch burst through the buildings and an icy fist come down upon the Legionnaires.

Cora collided with Charlie when she tried moving again. When her gaze shot up to see why, the life drained from her cheeks.

Blocking their path was Sullen Sprit-Spellborrow. Alongside him stood the *witch,* Mara Rouge.

Charlie tried to shove Cora away, but a noose of snow tore up from the ground and clasped around Cora's neck like a white snake. She gasped, and Charlie went still as stone.

The young witch curled her fingers through the air, tightening Cora's noose of snow and demonstrating the muscles of her magic. Cora's air slimmed. But she forced her attention to Mikal, Redson, and Angel being swarmed by Ruby Legionnaires and forced to their knees. John, Juniper, and Wade were dragged away through the hoard, but Frosty pounded his fists, breaking John free. Only the baker sprinted down the onyx road and disappeared around a bend.

He was pursued by Legionnaires.

Elowin could have stopped this. Cora's gaze drifted back to where Charlie had lowered to his knees in submission, the singer's worry-filled eyes stuck on the white serpent tight on Cora's neck.

A tear slipped from Cora's gray eyes as the rest of the Cord was dragged away.

"Release her," Charlie demanded of Sullen. "Release her now, or I'll sing a song you'll spend the remainder of your timestring wishing you never heard."

Sullen's solemn face cracked. He released a heavy, dark laugh. The young witch smiled also, and the noose loosened around Cora's throat. Cora inhaled a sharp breath and toppled to her knees, involuntarily bowing before the two. Charlie did not look afraid of them; he only watched Cora.

After all their seasons of being the most cunning, impossible-to-catch infiltrators in the Red Kingdom, Cora Thimble and Charlie Little had finally been caught.

There was no trial, no negotiation, no time waiting in the dungeons. Cora and Charlie were hauled through the dim tunnels below the palace without explanation. When Charlie tried to hum a tune, he was smacked. When Cora tried to kick the same Legionnaire for whacking Charlie, her wrists were yanked back and tied.

Charlie burst out laughing, stifling a flit of annoyance as he watched them tie the knot. "Afraid of a little Director-of-Tournaments-in-training, are we?" he taunted the Legionnaires. "I imagine she could take all of you down. Yes, you're certainly best off to tie her up."

Charlie's merry sarcasm was the only thing keeping Cora's heart from punching right through her chest as the Legionnaires shoved them toward a tall slat door, beyond which the buzzing murmur of voices turned the space alive.

Charlie did not know the layout of the palace well enough to realize where they were, but Cora would always know this place. She had put Greens—just like Charlie—before this very door. She had been at meetings where practices such as this one were organized. She had done a thing or three during her timestring that she wished she never had now that she was here.

Cora looked at Charlie, her partner of many seasons, her sharp gray eyes now pale. She hoped he would catch on to what was happening before the door was rolled open and they were shoved through. He did not deserve to be taken by surprise.

Charlie glanced back at her, but his eyes showed no such understanding. He whispered a quiet tune that drifted through the air. Cora felt it murmur across her very bones, cleansing the air in her lungs of its fears. She took in a deep breath of that song and let it out slowly.

Cora had escaped this fate for a good measure of seasons. But this was where it had all begun for the keymaker's daughter who had seen visions and dreamt dreams. She supposed it was fitting that it was where her journey would also end.

In the arena.

A Legionnaire tied a cloth around Charlie's mouth like a muzzle to silence his song.

THIRDLY

Mikal

The roar of voices was deafening, and Mikal felt the sound of it rush through his blood, burning him from the inside out. The crowd chanted indecipherable words as the tall door before him and Redson ripped open, and the Migraithe brothers were shoved out onto a snow-dusted floor beneath blinding lights.

The air glittered with snowflakes. Mikal blinked to try and see through the snow and lights, to perceive what was happening past the roaring voices.

Across a wide, oval arena the once-Legionnaire knew well, Mikal's blurry gaze settled on a figure with black-blue hair and silver neck tattoos being tossed to the floor like a lifeless doll. He heard Redson snarl from beside him, felt Redson try and take a step toward where Angel attempted to drag herself to her feet with her hands tied behind her back.

She must have put up a fight on the way in; her hair was tossed every which way and there was fire in her eyes.

Everyone was there. Everyone left in the Cord, except for Edward and John Dough.

Charlie and Cora were thrust in side-by-side—Charlie with fabric stuffed in his mouth. Juniper and Wade blinked up at the lights pulsing down from the stained-glass features in the dome. The pair moved timidly like young snow pups learning to walk for the first time. Two pegs out of their shells.

Only Mikal and Redson were left to try and keep everyone from being turned to snow in the next hour as they faced the cruelties of the Directors of Tournaments.

Mikal's flesh turned cold as a sweet scent drifted through the air like powdery roses and sour plums, and all thoughts of hope sank down his body. When he turned to look upon the face of the new presence in the arena, he wished he had never harvested a speck of hope to begin with.

The screams and cheers of the spectators elevated to fill the space, drowning out all other noise, including the thumps of the witch's heavy footsteps in her copper sabatons.

Mara Rouge, they called her. Citizen-proclaimed queen of the snow itself. Mikal had heard her name—though he had never dared to say it aloud.

"Ragnashuck," Redson muttered.

Mikal reached over his shoulder to a contraption holding his shepherd staff to his back. It seemed the Ruby Legion did not expect Mikal's walking stick to be a problem. He would make sure it was a problem.

The witch tilted her head, and long tendrils of maize hair slid over her shoulders. Her smile was just a pinch too wide, troubling for anyone with a soul left to fight for. She raised a long red nail and twirled it. The descending snowflakes re-directed their course, rushing on in a great, turbulent path in circles above. The current felt wrong—it whispered things in Mikal's ears:

Failure. Failure. Failure.

You are worth less than a handful of rings.

Mikal glanced at Redson to tell him to ignore the noise and realized Redson did not have his weapon. Mikal bit his lips shut. He had told his brother not to fight in the street.

So, it was just one Winter guardian against the witch, then.

Mikal slammed his staff against the arena floor, rattling the snow at his boots. Sharp points of ice materialized from the hook of his weapon. It caught the witch's attention, and she studied it with a blank look for a moment. Then, she stretched out her hands.

The spinning snow came rushing down like a flood.

It scathed Mikal's eyes with cold, repetitive stabs. He heard Redson cursing. Juniper screamed from across the arena, and Cora was yelling. Mikal pointed his staff at the witch, stealing the focus of the snow under her spell, and he sent it flying back at her.

It raged against the girl's cheeks, flipping her wild ten-drils of hair like a living creature of its own. She raised a hand, and half the snow obeyed, stopping in mid-air. She raised her other hand, and Mikal felt his hold on the snow slip.

It came back at him like a white spear. Mikal barely had time to slash it through before it would have met his throat. The witch stood straight, her pale blue eyes swimming with new rage. It seemed she had not expected much of a fight from the Cord of a Dozen Strands.

Then, a smile. A red, wicked one, slipping out from the corner of her mouth. A bone-shuddering laugh erupted, and she opened her arms wide. Metal rattled in the heights of the arena, and the stained-glass dome ceiling shattered, raining down glass upon the spectators who screamed and began to flee. But Mikal kept his sights on the witch. He reached deep within himself to those old sacred truths he had written. He murmured them aloud, feeling them strengthen his spirit. When he raised his staff and aimed, he fired with every last morsel of snow in the arena.

The witch was slapped back with a shriek. She slid over the floor and slammed into a pile of snow at the stage's edge, disappearing beneath the drift. Redson released a cheer, but those left in the raging crowd went silent.

Mikal marched after the girl using his staff as a walking stick, eying that pile so he might be ready when she got up. But he only made it halfway. His legs grew heavy and stiff, his feet coming to a halt on the snowy floor. His pumping blood turned icy in his veins, and he looked down with wide eyes to find an unnatural mist trickling over his feet, crawling up his calves, and reaching for the rest of him. He knew the rumours that said this witch could freeze the living to ice. He should have remembered.

The witch came bursting from the snow pile, dagger out, and she plunged it into his shoulder. Mikal's cooling heart tumbled off beat—snow spurted from within his body containing flecks of red blood. He could not even move his mouth to scream. He was ice.

When the witch tore the blade back out, she growled at

him with eyes that had turned as black as night. She tossed the dagger aside, and when she raised her hands, great limbs of snow reached down from the skies outside. They cracked like whips, striking Mikal's friends. They were all frozen, like him.

The arena had become a graveyard with ice statue gravestones, the Cord of a Dozen Strands marking the places where they would breathe their last.

FOURTHLY

Sullen Sprit-Spellborrow

As much as he had desired to watch Cora Thimble and her vocalist ally meet their fate in the arena, Sullen had been summoned to witness the negotiations between the Crimson Court and the one only fools called *Elowin*. If that was even his real name. It seemed rather self-indulgent to steal a name from ancient scripture and wear it like a crown of authority in the present.

The *Elowin* folk had rather remarkable eyes. Sullen found he could not look directly into them. He felt a twist in his stomach whenever he tried to gaze upon those colours that always seemed to be moving, bursting, growing brighter. It was a cheap trick of the light, and Sullen did not care for it.

Apart from the folk's magic eyes, Sullen did not find Elowin to be that impressive. He seemed an ordinary Rime

Folk. Ordinary hands, ordinary tanned flesh, ordinary bark-brown hair, ordinary Red Kingdom prison clothes.

The Crimson King sat off to the side in a plush chaise with his two oldest sons, letting the court handle the matter of the surrendered folk. There was a troubled speck on the king's brow though, weighing his expression down.

"You claim to be a king?" It was aged Hoff Merwinkle who spoke on behalf of the Reds. The man's white hair mirrored the snow shuffling against the windows. It seemed something nearby was stirring the air outside into a wicked storm.

"I am what I am. Those who choose to see me will recognize what I am without being told. Those who do not choose to see me will stay blind of their own accord." When Elowin spoke, Sullen was sure his blood warmed slightly at the sound. The folk always seemed to speak in parables or riddles. How frustrating.

"Why surrender then?" The Crimson King rasped the question from where he sat. "You eluded me for five full seasons. You turned half the villages against me. You could have raised an army and tried to take the palace."

Elowin looked at the Crimson King now, and it seemed the king of the Red Kingdom lost his voice the moment their gazes locked. "I do not want your throne, King."

Members of the Crimson Court exchanged glances. Some of them rolled their eyes. Lady Temptora released a snort-laugh and shoved a large berry in her mouth. Sullen watched the juices leak down her chin before she snatched a napkin to wipe it away.

"The sentence for your crimes will be *death!*" Hoff Merwinkle's cheeks turned pink. "You cannot claim to be *king* in another folk's kingdom."

"I agree." Elowin's words were soft.

"—You cannot *mislead* our villages. You cannot teach our people a *new way*. You shall be made an example of! You shall be turned to snow on a public tree where all can witness your fall. This is what happens to enemies of the Red Kingdom! What have you to say of this?!"

Elowin looked from one court member to the next. He did not seem afraid, and for that Sullen bristled. "I have not taught the folk a new way. I have reminded them of their first way. The one that was lost behind the noise." Elowin flicked his hands and the wires binding his wrists burst into a flurry of snowflakes and fell to the floor at his feet.

Crimson Court members gasped and shuffled—a folk or three ran around the table to put distance between themselves and the young man in the middle of the room.

"I offer myself freely as a sacrifice. You may turn me to snow on your public tree," said Elowin. Sullen could have sworn a breeze blew through the room. A trail of golden dust seemed to be left behind.

Hoff Merwinkle's eyes were round, but he settled back in his chair. "You are clearly a magician. And our restraints can't hold you. So, what do you have to gain by doing this?"

"I ask only for a trade," Elowin said, and the gold dust in the room settled.

A finger of blackness curled through Sullen's chest, and he stiffened his spine. It was not his place, but he stood to address this man, his spirit forcing him forward. A voice whispered in his ear—that master Sullen served. The scribe's slippers tapped over the tile floor. None of the Crimson Court stopped him, as though they had been instructed to be quiet.

Sullen came before Elowin. When Elowin looked back at him, Sullen felt a shudder in his body. For the first time, he looked into those eyes, and in them, he saw his own reflection. Sullen saw his straight nose, his thin lips, and his eyes…his once-yellow irises seemed to have turned black. He nearly staggered back at the sight, but something held his feet to the floor like heavy chains on his palace slippers.

"Elowin." The voice had come from Sullen's throat, but it did not sound like his voice. "Or shall I call you by your ancient names? Yule-child. Son of the White Kingdom. Christkind." Those names hung in the air, rippling through Sullen's soul like a gong being struck. "Bow to me, and I shall grant you half of this kingdom for your own purposes. You need not suffer and die."

Sweat broke out across Sullen's Rime flesh as Elowin stared. The scribe fought the impulse to vomit. When he glanced back at the court, he found them bent forward with their hands slapped over their ears as though a great, sharp noise rang through the room. Some of them cried out, but their shouts were silent. Sullen could not hear a thing apart from the conversation on his own mouth.

When Elowin did not offer a response, the voice made Sullen speak again. "Why surrender for *them*? They are unworthy. Don't you see? You are too powerful for their chains."

"Let's make a trade," Elowin said.

"A trade…" When the dark voice laughed it was deafening, and Sullen nearly slapped his own hands against his ears. Four sharp nails seemed to press into the sides of his mind, inching their way in, trying to crush him from the inside. "I will never spare Winter."

"Spare a single soul in the present. Give him and his offspring immunity to your witch's power."

"Just one soul? You would go through all this for just one of them?"

"Yes," Elowin said. "It all starts with one."

Sullen felt the sharp nails slide back out from his mind.

The Crimson Court were released from their hold. Members tumbled to the floor, some gasping, and Sullen found he could hear them again. But a word slipped from his mouth in that beastly tone, "Deal."

"Seize him! Bring him to the tree to be turned to snow before he uses his *trick* on us again!" Hoff Merwinkle pointed at Elowin with a trembling hand.

"What says the king?" A Legionnaire asked, drawing out a fresh rope but waiting for the king's command.

The Crimson King's black hair was ruffled. He looked upon the folk with the rainbows in his eyes, and after a moment or three, he marched over to the gold basin of drinking water. He dipped his hands into it and scrubbed furiously as the court watched, puzzled. When he was finished, the king reached for a silk cloth to dry his hands. He turned to face his court. "I wash my hands of this muddle. The court will decide what happens to this folk."

The Crimson King tossed the cloth to the table and left the room.

The court looked to Hoff with rosy cheeks. A crooked smile found the aged man, and he pointed a time again.

"Take him to the tree," he said.

Sullen felt the blackness slip out of his chest as he

watched Elowin be grabbed, rebound, and led from the court meeting room.

He stared after them, long after Elowin had disappeared from sight.

Sullen rubbed his chest, the first flit of fear he had felt in all his seasons rising to the surface.

FIFTHLY

Redson

The limbs of snow felt like fire on his skin. Redson could hardly breathe, could hardly think. The Cord of a Dozen Strands speckled the mostly empty arena where the crowds of Red nobles had left them to die. His fingers and toes had turned to frost, his throat crisping to ice. He felt his lungs freeze over.

The young witch did a violent dance, channelling the snow and suffocating them with it. Redson wished his eyes were frozen shut with the rest of him so he might not have to watch his end come rushing in. He wished he never saw the witch stab Mikal. Wished he had never witnessed Charlie Little silenced with a cloth gag. Wished he had never seen Angel Snow with her hair in knots.

But a flutter moved through Redson's slow heart. It was as though it had picked up a second beat. His breast pocket grew warm, heating his skin, and he found he could gasp—his lungs thawed.

"What in all of Winter..." he said against the raging snow. And then, "Ragnashuck!" when he realized he could speak.

He looked down with a loosened neck, feeling the frost leaking away from his body, sliding down his legs, and abandoning his toes. His pocket glowed, a golden light against the pure white sea.

Redson looked through the haze to Cora and Charlie frozen in place. Charlie's face was coated in a mask of ice, his lips darkening to blue. Past them, Angel's hair was lifted in a spray of solid navy curls like a frozen fountain.

Redson drew the orb from his glowing pocket. The cream and gold within it swirled, the colours leaking from the glass and printing words onto his fingers—*moving* words that rippled. It formed columns like the script on Mikal's shepherd staff. Redson felt the snow in the air turn its ear to listen.

With wide eyes, Redson raised a hand. The pocket of snow around him halted like it was told. And when Redson looked back at the witch commanding the arena, he *charged* at her.

With a mighty cry, Redson raised the glass ball in his fist to stop the snow attacking his allies and his brother. A startled look found the witch's face as he came sweeping from the storm in a glow of light. Her eyes flickered between pale blue and black. Suddenly, she laughed. She slapped a hand of snow across Redson's face, bringing him to a staggering stop.

"What did it cost your king, Carrier, for you to have this

gift?" she asked, and Redson's face changed. "You aren't worthy of his grace, or his sacrifice. You hardly believed in him when it mattered."

Her words drove ice into Redson's stomach. What did she mean, *"What did it cost your king?"* He glanced at his orb.

The witch's bellowing laughter boomed through his mind, filling him with doubt. It echoed along the rims of the empty arena.

"This marks the beginning. My first battle against the saints. But it will not be my last. I shall destroy you in the end." The voice that spoke was not that of a youthful girl anymore, but that of a monster. Redson choked and took a step back, suddenly unsure of what he was doing. Suddenly wondering why he had ever walked away from his life as an elite Legionnaire with everything he could have wanted at his fingertips.

He shook the thoughts from his head. They were not his.

"What is your name, monster?" he asked, swallowing his nerves and doubts.

The witch's head snapped to the side, her fingers curling in and out. "My name..." The girl's mouth twisted like she had eaten something sour. "I am the Night, made flesh."

"Night." Redson felt his tongue prickle as he spoke it. "Elowin must have had a reason."

Redson thrust a glowing, word-covered hand forward, and a wall of snowflakes tore up from the ground, driving against the witch and wrapping her like a blanket. It lifted her right off the arena floor and took her through the hole in the glass ceiling. Redson pushed and pushed and *pushed* until the witch disappeared over the roof's edge, her raging screams vanishing along with her.

Redson tumbled to his knees. The sound of Mikal falling from his freeze spell was a sweet song in his ears. He spun to find all the members of the Cord moving, panting for air. Charlie rushed to untie the wires binding Cora's wrists, and Wade picked Juniper up off the floor.

Angel ran to where Mikal buckled forward with a hand gripping his shoulder. Blood and snow drifted down his black jacket and speckled the floor.

"Get the dagger and cut Angel's ties. We need to escape while the arena is empty," Mikal rasped, dragging over his shepherd staff and reattaching it to the contraption on his back.

Redson fetched the cold dagger the witch had used and sliced Angel's wires in one sweep. Angel helped Mikal stand, and Redson took the rest of his brother's weight.

"By the sharpest wind, Redson, what in all of Winter happened? How did you do that?" Angel asked as they rushed to where Cora was pulling Juniper toward the doors.

"Something is happening with Elowin," Redson said. "We need to hurry. I think they're about to turn him to snow."

SIXTHLY

Edward

The once-prince's heart pounded. He watched Reds drag Elowin through the Scarlet City toward that horrid public tree at the top of the hill where a thousand plus ten thousand could witness his death. Edward and Gathadriel remained hidden, watching from the tea shop roof.

The air reeked with the smell of gnome flesh. Edward had learned since leaving Green that the gnomes were an army of creatures living below the Red Kingdom, summoned only for times such as these. They were the brutes who carried out the Reds' vilest assignments.

Plums were hurled at Elowin, insults were flung, and folk standing by poked at him with their strolling sticks.

"Why is he letting them do this, Gathadriel?" Edward whispered, a silver tear cooling his hot cheeks.

"I cannot offer my opinions, Edward. You know this,"

Gathadriel said, but the fairy's dark brows were tipped inward, the corners of his mouth pulling down.

"Can we get closer? I want him to see me. I want Elowin to know we're here, at least." Edward traced his fingers up and down the wood toggles of his coat. His numb, restless spirit screamed in silence at this kingdom for being so blind to what they were doing to their True King.

Gathadriel nodded. They slipped into the skies, blending into the clouds, and they dropped on the hill where the Ruby Legion ushered Elowin to the tree. No Reds heard the thud of Gathadriel's sabatons amidst the shouting and ridicule in the streets. The Green prince and the fairy tucked themselves behind a ruby statue to witness what would happen.

The public tree glistened with fresh snow, its branches curling up toward the foggy sky. Edward watched the Ruby Legionnaires tug Elowin to it.

Elowin glanced right at Edward. The True King of Winter did not look afraid. In fact, the purple hues in his eyes did a merry dance.

"He knows," the once-prince whispered to Gathadriel. "He knows we're with him."

Gathadriel nodded as his only response, the fairy's thin wings fluttering at his back as the Legionnaires tied Elowin's limbs to the tree.

"Wait," Edward whispered. He took a step forward. "Is that…" A wreath he recognized all too well was carried to the tree by a Legionnaire with a sneer upon his mouth. It was the crown given as a gift to Elowin by a woman-folk after her babe had been healed in the street; a symbol from the first day Elowin had shown himself in the Red Kingdom.

"A crown for a king," the Legionnaire said in utter

mockery.

Had it not been for Gathadriel snatching Edward by the belt, Edward might have charged the tree as the Legionnaire placed the wreath atop Elowin's head. The branches pierced Elowin's temples, and a glistening tear of blood ran down his cheek. Still, Elowin did not react, shout, or rebel.

"Gathadriel…" Edward croaked, placing a fist against his mouth so he would not scream.

The crown had been a *gift*, now used as a slap of humiliation.

A low rhythm lifted through the crowd, and a palace musician moved to the front with a drum in his grip. He beat against it with a branch—another mockery; a death song performed with another one of Elowin's treasures. A song for the king they rejected. The musician tossed the drum at Elowin's feet where the True King's blood would sprinkle down and paint it red.

A man with snow-white hair and hateful eyes emerged from the howling crowd. His gold nameplate read: HOFF MERWINKLE. The man carried a four-pointed iron star. It was the last piece of the Triad of Signs Elowin had created in Room Four Hundred Plus Six. The Triad had released the first breath of hope into all of Winter, far beyond the Red Kingdom. Edward could not imagine how the Reds had discovered it, or how they had gotten their hands on it. But here it was—the very tool they would use to destroy Elowin.

Hoff Merwinkle dropped the star to the ground and a gnome brought his heavy club down upon it, smashing it into four pieces which were gathered and carried to where Elowin was restrained.

Edward recoiled as the gnomes held the points of the star

against Elowin's hands and feet like nails. The Green prince spun away, clutching his stomach. Gathadriel closed his eyes.

There was noise, illness, and rebellion in Edward's heart as he waited for it to be over. He hated them. He hated the Reds. He would find a way to crush them all. Perhaps he would return to his kingdom, take back his throne, and meet the Crimson King in battle after all. Perhaps he would—

A soft, sweet song drifted through the Winter air, tickling Edward's ears, and his thoughts settled. He opened his eyes and wondered for a moment if Charlie Little was nearby. It sounded like one of the choir director's hymns.

When Edward turned back with tears chilling his cheeks, it took him searching a face or three before he spotted the other Green hiding in plain sight. On a nearby hill stood the members of the Cord of a Dozen Strands. Just a snowball's-throw away.

Charlie's song was low and quiet, travelling a great distance and comforting Edward's soul, as it reached Elowin's tree. A tribute—a *real* song for a real king. The deaf Reds carried on shouting and laughing and throwing their plums.

Sullen Sprit-Spellborrow appeared, clutching an ink pen with white knuckles. The scribe's yellow eyes were no more. Instead, pure black stones were his irises. With his back turned to the crowd, none could see his morphed features.

Sullen moved to the tree, waving away the gnomes.

A dark, chilling voice came from the scribe's mouth that affronted Edward's spirit. "Even Winter cannot save you from this death," it said.

Gathadriel's golden eyes narrowed on the scribe, the flittering of his wings coming to a halt.

The ink pen in Sullen's hand stabbed forward like a knife, piercing Elowin's side, and Gathadriel growled, drawing the attention of Reds in the crowd.

"The folk you chose to save has no offspring. And I shall destroy him before he produces any," the beastly voice promised in a whisper. Sullen tore the ink pen back out and Elowin's body sagged, but he did not use his power to save himself. His blood spilled down upon the drum and the snow below.

Gathadriel lifted Edward from the hill as nearby Reds became curious of them. But Edward still heard what was said next.

The True King whispered one last thing as Sullen's gaze dropped to Elowin's belt where a set of multicoloured metal keys were fastened on a ring. Sullen slapped his empty pocket in surprise.

"You think you're only fighting my flesh and blood, Nightflesh," he said. "But someday, I will return."

SEVENTHLY

Mikal

Every grain and flake of creation told a story. Mikal had heard the stories since his early seasons while picking white apples alongside his brother. But he had never heard a tale quite like the one that Winter screamed when its painter, its True King, took his last breath.

Thousands of folk had come to witness Elowin be turned to snow. The Cord of a Dozen Strands stood at a distance, holding hands and lifting each other up until the moment it was finished.

From the dark streams below the kingdom, a great roar of victory sounded; a deafening chant that reverberated over the Scarlet City and made certain Rime Folk jump. But that cry of darkness was silenced by the groan of Winter. The angry roar of the snowseas far across Winter's plains. The crackling rebellion of the skies as they thundered above with flashes of colour and light. The grumbling of the Glass Mountains who called out to their king. Stars shot across the daylight skies, and a legion of white birds burst through the branches of the public tree, snapping twigs and making the nearest Rime Folk shriek in alarm. The songbirds' bellowing calls filled the city so that all would hear and know that Elowin had been the True King from the beginning. The one whom they rejected even though Winter itself had known. Creation knows its own maker.

Elowin did not turn back into snow, for it was not from snow that he was weaved together. His body dissolved into a pile of golden dust that was taken up by a gust of wind before anyone could get close enough to touch it. The birds sang at a volume unheard of in Winter past, filling the skies with glory and praise as though Elowin was now among them.

Cora said a thing that reminded the Cord of a Dozen Strands where they were as they stared at the glory around them.

"It's time for you to gather your sputtlepuns and flee, Mikal and Redson," she said. "I imagine John went to look after them at the inn when he escaped. But those boys and girls *must* run now. That Beast who commands the witch will be coming for them next."

Mikal looked to Redson at his left and Angel at his right, the two of them holding him up entirely. His blood stained Angel's deep blue hair in patches. He was leaking all over the place.

"Ragnashuck..." he whispered, swallowing his emotions. He could not imagine leaving now, leaving Elowin's death behind.

"Cora's right, brother. We need to get our sputtlepuns out of here." Redson turned their trio toward the inn which was at least half the city away.

Cora's hand came up to stop them. "Charlie and I will get your young folk to Room Four Hundred Plus Six to stay a night, and we'll meet you past the iron gates on tomorrow's eve. You won't make it to the tavern in your condition, Mikal. Charlie and I will get the young ones. You can trust us to do it. You three head for the gate and slip out when you can."

Mikal and Redson exchanged a glance.

Suddenly, a low, beastly voice rippled over the Scarlet City wind, weaving a new, shuddering story into Mikal's bones. Mikal was not sure how he heard it, but it filled his blood with ice and terror, and when he looked at Redson, he knew his brother had heard it too.

"To all who hear my commands: Assemble the armies of Red and find Redson Migraithe."

EIGHTHLY

Cora

In the dimness of night, a measure of sputtlepuns crept along, following the glow of the tin lantern in Cora's grip. Charlie walked at the back of the group, humming along, batting away the dark spirits in the air, along with John Dough who kept a fidgety eye about.

The young ones were a feisty bunch, filled with giggles and toots and twiddlings and songs. But they all understood the importance of their silence now. Not a peep came from the youths as they rounded the corner to Room Four Hundred Plus Six.

Cora lifted the lantern to the door, taking in a deep breath and hoping that none had discovered their beloved room while they were gone. With no keys left to lock it, the door had remained unlocked for nearly five full seasons. Open to any and all who might come looking for it.

Cora pushed the door wide and ushered the young ones inside. Many looked around curiously, but in a pinch they forgot their manners and spread about the rooms, snooping through drawers. The ones in white pulled the glass orbs from their pockets to light the way through the halls until Charlie lit a fire in the living area so all could see and get warm.

Cora closed the door and leaned back against it, dragging a hand through her fair hair. She rewatched that moment in her mind's eye of rushing to the hill and spotting Elowin being nailed in place by the shattered star. She had known it would happen. She had seen it in a dream.

Still, she had not been ready.

Only the chuckles and banter seeping from the living area warmed her soul and heart, reminding her of all she had been fighting for. Charlie appeared in the hall doorway. He did not need to say a thing. His presence was soothing enough. Though times were troubling, he cast her a smile.

Cora found herself smiling back. She did not even know why when there were ten plus eight boys in raven-black filling the living area along with ten plus eight sputtlepuns in white playing catch with their glowing orbs.

"What a quarter it's been, Green," she said across the foyer.

She wondered if Charlie would suggest they leave with the rest of the Cord and never come back to the Red Kingdom. But even though portions of their fight had come to an end with Elowin gone, Cora knew she was not finished. She had never felt called to leave the Red Kingdom behind, even now. She could not abandon those she grew up with, those living in the palace still. She could not abandon the souls still to be saved within these kingdom borders.

She dragged her gaze from Charlie to the cold tea kettle. Her sharp gray eyes narrowed in on a thing sitting atop the table, glimmering in the dim light of the living area, and a patter rose in her chest.

Sitting atop the table was a large metal ring of keys in various shapes, sizes, and colours.

"Ragnashuck..." She used the word of the Migraithe's by accident. But she could not believe what she was seeing and what it meant. "I think he's alive."

NINTHLY

Redson

It had taken two days to escape through the iron gate as it had been so heavily guarded by the Legion. The brothers had fashioned disguises for Angel, Juniper, and Wade out of burlap sacks, red ribbons stolen off a flower cart, and blossoms lifted off a store porch.

Redson and Mikal's disguises were a pinch more clever than that. They had waited until a burly pair of Legionnaires were slumped over in fitful sleep outside the vapour houses, and the brothers had stolen their crimson capes and swords. Redson even snatched an extra sword for Angel. He had offered it to her with a lighthearted wink, certain he would win her heart one day.

Even with their hoods up, no one questioned the Migraithe brothers when they looked to be Ruby Legionnaires searching for the enemy who was, *"to be found and brought to the palace at all costs,"* according to the latest release of the Pebble Paper.

The Cord had slid past the gate one-by-one. Mikal had healed enough to inhale a deep breath without trouble though he could barely hold his shepherd staff without terrible pain.

The iron gates glistened at their backs as they regrouped and travelled as a pack of five into the dense valleys of snow rimming the kingdom. Redson found he liked having a sword again. It had been a merry measure since he had carried a weapon of his own, apart from his staff and his glass orb.

But as they came over the second hill, the brothers realized what waited for them on the other side.

Redson released a slow, heavy huff. "I knew it was too easy."

Gnomes spotted the white hills in scratched armour, their clubs and swords at the ready. Fair-fleshed Greed drew long bows, and icicles formed in their fingers as they pulled on the strings, ready to fire at the one they had been instructed to kill. Ruby Legionnaires stood side-by-side in a line before them all. Their numbers were in the hundreds, possibly thousands.

"Edward's ice caves are not far from here. They're just past the dunes. We could run for it and maybe find a snow pirate willing to trade for passage—"

"And lead this Red army right to Edward?" Redson asked, interrupting Juniper.

"What about the dwarves? They have a cabin just around the frost giants' valley. If we can make it there—"

"My dear friend," Redson said, facing Juniper and taking her tenderly by her shoulders. "This army is not here for you. They are here for me. And as shameful as my brother would think it, I admit, I have been craving a fight with the

Ruby Legion for a good measure. I will not lead this army to Edward. I will not lead this army to the dwarves. I will not lead this army to you. And I will certainly not lead this army to the rest of the sputtlepuns," he said, and Juniper's face fell as she seemed to gather what he was saying.

"Redson," Mikal said, dragging his shepherd staff from his back. "I will fight with you."

"No, brother. Your sputtlepun guardians need to protect my Carriers. We have done too much work to lose them now. One of us must live through this day, and we already know it will not be me." Redson drew his sword. He put a hand on his brother's shoulder.

A tear spilled down Mikal's rosy cheek.

"I will try to hold back this army while you flee. But they will get past me. Brother, get our friends away before that happens. Tell the sputtlepuns our story when you meet up with Cora and Charlie again," Redson said.

Mikal's buttery-gold eyes were dismal and filled with objections. But he nodded.

The sound of a second sword being drawn filled the hilltop. Redson realized Angel was preparing for battle, pushing up her jacket sleeves and tying her hair into a long blue braid. She glanced at him, brow raised. "You got me a sword, didn't you? I'd be a scotchy friend if I didn't use it." Angel Snow began marching down the hill in her boots, ready to take on the army alone if Redson did not catch up. A touch of warmth filled his chest, and he smiled. But Redson looked back at his brother one last time.

Mikal exhaled a long, shaky breath. This would not be easy for him, Redson knew. The brothers had fought alongside each other for all their seasons.

"I will see you in the White Kingdom, brother," Redson said. "Learn to talk a measure more. You're painfully stuffy when you're quiet," he said. Redson turned to march after Angel before she could collide with the Ruby Legion alone and steal all the glory.

As he approached, a great, growling cheer erupted from the Red army. The Greed slinked around the gnomes and crept up the hill, their white eyes on those Redson had left behind. Redson glanced back to make sure his friends were leaving and sent a silent prayer into the air, praying that those dwarves guarding the sputtlepuns back at Mikal's library and Wentchester Cove were up for a fight.

Redson reached Angel's side just as every sort of evil swept across the valley toward them.

"Don't be afraid," he said, which brought Angel to look at him with that same raised brow as before. She offered him her stunning smile which he would think about until his last breath on this field.

"I'm not afraid, Redson Migraithe. I'm certain this is the moment I was created for."

Their eyes were for each other as the Red army closed in, Legionnaire and gnome alike. And when Redson and Angel broke their gaze to lift their swords, they put up a fight unlike any recorded on a Winter timestring. They fought flesh and bone, sword and shield, might and muscle. They made the Ruby Legion regret coming into the fields.

It was a true season's miracle. Both held a smile of satisfaction in the moment when their Rime flesh was turned back into snow.

LASTLY, AND SO FORTH

Charlie

Funny things often happened to Charlie Little. Silly, odd things. And though recent times had tossed him for a spin, Charlie stood on the cliffside beside his best friend, Edward Haid, and gazed down upon the valley called Wentchester Cove, feeling rather giddy about it all.

After Charlie, Cora, and John had escorted the sputtlepuns home—a journey that had taken a full day plus one half—they had learned that a band of merry dwarves had fought off two hundred plus thirty Greed in the mountains. Charlie had blinked, and blinked, and blinked a time again.

"Dwarves?" Edward had laughed so hard at the unexpectedness of it, the once-prince had tipped forward and soaked the knees of his pants.

The ten plus eight Carriers of Truth were reunited with the rest of the sputtlepuns Redson had gathered and taught in his past five seasons. The flock of white-cloaked youth nearly filled half the valley. Their orbs glowed when they went in and out of the tunnel in the cliff, chatting amongst themselves of the news that Redson Migraithe, their beloved teacher, had taken on an entire Red army. The rumour grew each time it was repeated, and Charlie could have sworn he overheard one of the young folk claim Redson had, "punched ten plus two gnomes at once and turned them all to snow dust in one blow."

Charlie had grinned at that.

All right. He had started that rumour himself.

At the valley's edge, Mikal appeared with a great multitude of boys in raven-black carrying hooked shepherd staffs. Their colours were a clean contrast to the paleness of the snow. From a distance, Mikal nodded up to his two friends on the cliffside who were eavesdropping on the sputtlepuns.

A folk approached Charlie's shoulder. By the soft clinking of metal keys in her dress pocket, he knew who it was even before she slid her hand into his. When Charlie looked at Cora, he noticed her eyes were the same colour as the clouds today: perfect. *Perfect* would always be Cora's colour to him.

Juniper, Wade, John, and even Gathadriel joined them on the cliffside, watching as Mikal led the guardians into the mix of white coats.

"More of us will die," Edward said at Charlie's side now that they were all together. "I imagine all of us will in the end. That Beast will hunt us to the edges of the snow globe for all we've done."

"Perhaps," Cora agreed. But she took in a deep breath of Winter air, and Charlie found that she was smiling. "But even so, we're going to raise a generation to fight like the globe has never known."

Charlie felt that promise lift into a song, sliding through the trees that ruffled in the wind, dancing along the drifts of snow, and bursting into the hearts of the Carriers of Truth who filled the valley. The ones who would bring the merry news of great hope into all the darkest corners of Winter.

The offspring of Redson Migraithe.

THE END
OF
CAROLS AND SPIES
COLLECTION, THE FIRST

Just a few thanks…

Thank you to my editor, Melissa Cole, for being the best and for working so hard on my books.

Thank you to my Patrons: Sarah Breed, Danielle, Lyndsey Hall, Redlac (Jesse), and Kanyon Kiernan. You guys keep me going! (To become one of my Patrons and be involved in what I'm doing, visit my website!)

Thank you to everyone who has bought my books, left a review, and spread the word about The Winter Souls Series. This book series has changed my life.

And lastly, thank **you** for reading Carols and Spies!

OTHER BOOKS BY JENNIFER KROPF

A SOUL AS COLD AS FROST
A HEART AS RED AS PAINT
A CROWN AS SHARP AS PINES
A BEAST AS DARK AS NIGHT

Made in United States
North Haven, CT
21 January 2024

47714987R00181